S0-CAB-787

"A STRONG, COMPELLING NOVEL. . . . The plot is believable, the characters sharply drawn, the prose clean and distinctive." —*The Washington Post*

"POWERFUL . . . PACED AT EXPRESS SPEED . . . A PAGE-TURNER. A highly readable account of a war whose losses American writers continue to count."
—*Chicago Tribune Book World*

IN VIETNAM YOU LEARNED TO CONGRATULATE THE WOUNDED AND FORGET THE DEAD. IT MIGHT TAKE EVERYTHING YOU HAD TO MOURN FOR THOSE WHO HAD SURVIVED.

# Fragments

A Novel by

## JACK FULLER

"A FIRST-RATE WAR NOVEL and a penetrating and successful effort to understand America's involvement in Vietnam. . . . There are times when you feel you are reading a thriller." —*The Wall Street Journal*

"AN AMBITIOUS, TIGHTLY CONTROLLED NOVEL THAT MAKES THE USUAL . . . ACCOUNT . . . SEEM FLIMSY. . . . Mr. Fuller has succeeded, with Neumann, in creating a figure of mythic dimensions. . . . Shapeliness and sense of larger design [is] elegantly executed in *Fragments*." —*The New York Times*

*By the same author*

CONVERGENCE

# Fragments

# Jack Fuller

A DELL BOOK

Published by
Dell Publishing Co., Inc.
1 Dag Hammarskjold Plaza
New York, New York 10017

Dell ® TM 681510, Dell Publishing Co., Inc.

ISBN: 0-440-12687-8

Reprinted by arrangement with William Morrow and Company, Inc.

Printed in the United States of America

February 1985
10 9 8 7 6 5 4 3 2

WFH

*For my father and mother*

There was the law, he said.
Nature had given him a sign.

—STEPHEN CRANE
*The Red Badge of Courage*


Wise men have always construed
the recognition of necessity as a
moment of freedom.

—PAUL RICOEUR
*Freedom and Nature*

# ACKNOWLEDGMENTS

Many people have helped me with this novel along the way. Early on, Robert Penn Warren gave me encouragement and advice on the manuscript. John Dystel, Seth Lipsky, Phil McCombs, Elliot Brown, Steve Yaffe and Tom Belt were there at the start urging me on. Edward Levi and his family have been a steady source of encouragement. Tim O'Brien, Bernard Weinraub, Norval Morris, Michael Kilian, John Twohey and Warren Spencer made helpful suggestions at a later stage. Peter Shepherd and his assistant, Wendy Schmalz, worked with the manuscript line by line and kept me going. My wife, Alyce, and son, Timothy, deserve more than just acknowledgment. They are the heart of everything.

# 1

# Neumann

You didn't really start noticing things again until the very end. The strange smell of the place, like spice on bad meat. The way the barbed wire moaned in the wind.

You climbed aboard a truck and rode through the countryside for the last time. And you finally opened your eyes to it, as if you were coming up from under a mortar barrage, lifting your face warily off the ground, blinking out the dust. This is what you saw: figures in conical hats moving through the paddies on line, as riflemen might, except that when you looked closely they were only women tending the rice. Ramshackle villages thrown together from material too worthless for war. Fields pocked by craters, and children playing in the pools that formed there.

You saw things you had never expected. Buddhist pagodas gaily lavished with bright icons and odd, unsovereign flags. Flame trees as delicate as garlands. Little children at the side of the road, waving and laughing and shouting "OK! OK! OK!" as if you were the first soldier on earth. Or the last. And despite everything, despite the numbness, despite the whole wasted year you had spent closing your eyes to these things, suddenly they blossomed out before you, as sad and beautiful as the fragile, momentary flowers in a rain forest.

Then you arrived at your destination, the last stop before you got on the airplane they said would set you free. You threw your duffel bag on an empty bunk; you paced back and forth. You examined your hands, how dark and hard they had become, your heart. Day after day you fell into formation and heard them call the names of other men for their flights. But the names meant nothing. The men meant nothing. You were putting everything behind you, or at least you were trying to, in your head.

But still in the dark you could hear the artillery firing in the distance, indifferent as thunder, and you worried whether the rounds would land short. You could hear foreign voices chattering in the night, and you craned your neck to hear what they said and wondered whether it was true. You tried to make connections. Nothing fancy. The simple things. Chronology. Cause and effect. When did each man die and how? It was hard just to get even that much straight. But you kept at it anyway. You had to. You were going home.

Barnelli sat on the edge of his bunk sorting a stack of wilted letters into piles. Now and then he brought one up to his nose and sniffed.

"Stink of the paddies turn you on?" said Daniels.

"Sweet smell she put on them," said Barnelli. "I hoped some of it would still be left."

"She ain't gonna like the way you smell," said Daniels.

"It washes off. Don't it, Morgan?"

"How the hell should I know?" I said.

Daniels leafed through a fresh copy of a skin magazine he had picked up somewhere. I leaned over to have a look. *Girls of the World* it was called.

"You think that's some kind of catalog?" I said.

"Don't be worrying about me in the World," he said. "I'll get my share."

"Fuckit," said Barnelli, looking down at the collection of letters from his girl.

"What's wrong?" I asked.

"Don't feel nothin'. That's what."

"There it is," said Daniels.

"Don't feel hungry," Barnelli chanted. "Just had chow."

"There it is," said Daniels, the sole congregation.

"Can't sleep. Can't think. Can't *even* shit. All stopped up every which way."

"There it is."

"Don't feel good."

"Tell it, brother. Tell the fool why."

"I'm still here, ain't I?"

We had been waiting for two days. The hootch had filled up and then it had emptied. All the others had been called for a flight: all the chair-borne clerks and cashiers, mechanics and musicians, mess sergeants and magicians, the whole damned carnival they sent to fight this war. And the only

15

ones left were the grunts. We always got the ass end.

Or else maybe it was just the odds at work again, those hard, mortal numbers that had been keeping score on us all year. A roll of the dice. Maybe the odds explained why we were still here instead of on our way home, just as they explained why we had lived to be here at all. Chances were one in three a straightleg infantryman would suffer a wound. But it could have been worse. Door gunners took twice as many hits. The pilot of a light observation helicopter lasted an average of seven months, a sniper eight and a half. The risk of an ambush depended on the time and terrain. We could put a figure on any variation. You might think that these numbers we lived by were nothing more than a hunch. But when a man was wounded, we could make a sound bet on life or death just by looking at his eyes. The numbers were that powerful.

Outside the hootch an old woman shuffled across the hot dirt yard carrying a scrawny chicken by its legs. It was getting on toward dusk, but the fever of the day had not yet broken. Big thunderclouds built behind her in the west, turning and rolling in Michelangelo colors.

"Lookit," said Daniels. "Nature's Jive Light Show."

The mama-san put the chicken down and squatted next to it. It kicked up puffs of red dust, trying to break free of the wire binding its legs. The old woman drew out a knife, rubbed it against the black silk at her calf. On my bunk I kicked up my feet a couple of times as if they were tied together.

16

"Crazy motherfucker," said Daniels.

The bright blade flashed in the sun as the mama-san honed it. Then she took the chicken by its head and stretched its neck out long. For some reason I turned away.

When it was done, the mama-san stood up, arranged herself, wiped off the knife and carried the carcass away. I looked out past her to where a group of big yellow buildings stood on a hill. They were the home of Headquarters, U.S. Army Vietnam.

"Hey, Daniels," I said.

"What you want now?"

"Ever been up there to USARV?"

"Don't no grunts go there."

"I've been there."

"I been up to my nose in this shit for a year, Morgan, but that don't mean everybody want to hear me go on about how it smelled."

I stood stiffly and limped to the door, where I could get a better look. I could not make out just which building we had gone to for the inquiry.

"You get fucked up, Morgan?" said Barnelli.

"Why?"

"Gimpy leg," he said. "You been acting funny."

"Some shrapnel in my hip is all. Tightens up on me sometimes."

Barnelli put all the letters down on his bunk, stood up and came over to me. He put his hand on my elbow.

"Let me tell you something," he said softly, hopefully. "If you don't get fucked up, I mean fucked up bad, a year here don't mean nothin'. Don't mean nothin' at all."

"There it is," said Daniels.

It was one of those things you said to one another for comfort, one of those things you really wanted to believe. A guy in another unit got greased. Don't mean nothin'. A round pierced your canteen and at first you weren't sure whether the dark stain spreading across your fatigues was water or blood. Don't mean nothin'. You survived, didn't you? Don't mean nothin' at all.

That was one of the things you said. Here was another: The odds are the same on every roll of the dice. Roll a seven today. Roll a seven tomorrow. It's the same every time you pick up the bones.

And another: It's just the way it's got to be.

And they all added up to the same thing. Chance and necessity. That was all there was to it. As much as you hated the odds, hated all the brute, amoral powers of the jungle, you had to cling to them. They left no room for blame.

The colonel's office at USARV had been all done up with combat watercolors on the walls and armchairs in the corners. We were definitely out of place—a raggedy-assed bunch of grunts. You could tell that the colonel thought so as he lined us up in front of his desk and looked us up and down.

"This is an informal inquiry, men," he said, checking out the sorry condition of our boots. "You may stand at ease."

He had on metal-rimmed glasses much too shiny to wear in the bush. And his skin had an even tan I just knew did not leave off where his starched jungle fatigues started. Two ashtrays, polished brass shell casings, sat squared away on either side of

18

his desk, and directly in front of him was a stack of papers. Beyond the windows, beyond the scraped red valleys and the wire, the jungle was a dark smear.

"Army policy," he said, "requires an inquiry into all unexplained civilian fatalities such as those reported in Xuan The. We are primarily interested in the circumstances surrounding the deaths of three members of the Le family and of an unidentified fourth victim, male Vietnamese type. Preliminary investigation indicates that all were killed by shots from an M-sixteen rifle issued to Sergeant James Neumann."

"They're out to get him," Thompson whispered.

"Nothing of the sort," the colonel snapped back. "There may be very good reasons for what happened. There often are. And we are here to find out about them. But I want to be clear about this. We are not concerned with war stories. I'm sure you are all some kind of heroes, but save it for the ladies back on the block. We are only concerned here with the ambiguous deaths."

When he called Neumann into the office, I was sickened by what I saw. He hobbled in on two canes, dragging a bad leg. His face was drawn tight across the bone. He had lost so much weight that it was remarkable he had the strength to walk at all. His hand shook as he leaned one cane against the front of the colonel's desk and gave a salute. But I had almost prepared myself for the physical part. Nobody took hits the way he had and came out whole, not even Jim Neumann. What made me shudder was the way he acted, as though none of us were there. I tried to sneak him

19

an encouraging look to reassure him that nothing I was going to say would hurt him. But he would not acknowledge it. And when I looked into his eyes, they were as empty as a blind man's.

I was not the only one who was shaken. Every one of us saw something of himself in Neumann—the best part, magnified. I will tell you how bad it was. When the inquiry was over and we drove back to the base camp, no one even spoke of it.

The colonel isolated Neumann in another office and then took each of us in turn while the others waited outside. He began with Thompson because Thompson was the one who had gotten the whole thing started. As soon as the platoon had returned to Quan Loi from the firefight, Thompson had gone into his usual routine. He strutted around, bragging up what had finally happened at our fool little pacification project. He got a little drunk, embellished the story, gave Neumann credit for finally wising up about the dinks. I am sure he did not expect all his bullshit would get back to the command, but it did somehow. And pretty soon the investigators were all over our case.

His testimony wasn't going to be much, though. He had been a long way from the only action that mattered. He could tell the colonel how we had gone in at dawn to secure a chopper that had been shot down. He could tell him about the ville, the way Neumann had adopted it and set about rebuilding a dispensary there. He would be glad to give a blow-by-blow description of the firefight that erupted on us. But he could not say what happened in the hootch. Nobody could do that except Neumann. I was the closest to him at the time, and I was a hundred yards away.

I don't know how the others handled it, but I gave it to the colonel straight. I told him exactly what I had witnessed the morning of the firefight. I did not leave out how Neumann had saved my ass. I did not fail to mention the machine gun and mortars, the way it had ended as well as the way it had begun. And if that was just a war story, then maybe the colonel needed to realize that it wasn't so easy to separate things out.

After we had all had our say, the colonel called us in to witness Neumann's testimony. It was the one part of the tale we had not been able to rehearse, and we all needed to hear it. We needed for him to lay it all out plain so that we would know for sure that he had only done what he had to do. We wanted to see the colonel squirm under the rude truth of it and be forced to admit that there wasn't anything more ambiguous about a death than about the trajectory of a shell. There was no great moral issue here, no infraction of the military code. It had been necessary, that's all. Necessary. We all wanted to believe that, and Jim Neumann was the man who could tell it. No matter how weak he seemed, we just knew that he could.

But he refused. Flat refused to answer any questions. He just shook his bowed head and never even looked up.

"Shit, man," said Thompson. "You got to defend yourself."

"The man does have certain rights," said the colonel, and we hated him for it.

Then he shuffled through his papers, had a short conversation in whispers with his aide and announced that the evidence of unjustified use of deadly force in Xuan The was inconclusive. He was actually smiling when he said it.

"Men," he said, "I want to thank you for your cooperation and to remind you that what you have said here has been under oath. If there is anything anyone wants to add, you had damned well better do it now." He paused, but not for long. "I am going to close the file. Sergeant Neumann, you will be released for evacuation to a hospital near your home. Based on what has been said here, I don't think we have a problem at all."

Only the personal problem, the kind the army won't attend to. If your wife sued for support, if your creditors started to squeeze, if your piss burned like acid, the army had ways of taking care of you. But if you woke up sweating in the middle of the night or if the sound of a rifle brought tears to your eyes, you just kept it to yourself because the army did not meddle in that kind of business. Neumann's emptied clip in the dust near the corpses. The shattered dispensary. The hootch afire. All the ambiguous deaths. Personal problem.

And so you nursed that problem through another night, and in the morning they finally called your name for a flight. You rode the bus past the faded yellow and brown hootches, over the red dirt ruts, past guard towers, scallops of sandbag bunkers, long Palmer spirals of barbed wire. At the end of the road the *Freedom Bird* sat bright and silver on the tarmac. You filed in, found a seat, listened to the big engines straining against the brakes. Then, finally, you were up and off. But still . . . still the land was under you, and so you did not quite relax. The little villages with their rusted iron roofs. The Black Virgin Mountain off in the haze. The shadow of the jet swimming in the dark green waves of the jungles below.

Then in a few minutes you were out over the South China Sea. The beaches of Vietnam slipped out of sight. You sat back in your seat, and a sigh shuddered through the cabin like a death rattle.

When I was laid up in the hospital after the firefight in Xuan The, I bought myself one of those little metal shaving mirrors so that I could keep an eye on my wounds. A regular mirror was out. They were worried about my attitude. No glass. No razors. No belt on my robe. They didn't like the fact that I wasn't laying down the usual line of bullshit. They said I was withdrawn all out of proportion to the severity of my injury.

Just before they took me into surgery to dig out the last, deepest fragments, the doctor stopped by my bed.

"They tell me you're keeping a pretty good eye on yourself," he said, consulting the charts hanging from the foot of my bed. I didn't say anything. It wasn't a question.

"Once we go in there today and pull out the rest of it," he said, "I think you'll begin to see an improvement. You know, there's nothing much for you to worry about. You just got some shrapnel in the tush. That's all. It could have been worse. Your tush is pretty much just fatty tissue and muscle. The only thing important is the hole."

"Listen," I said. "You want to do me a favor, Doc?"

"Sure," he said, leaning in on me. "Anything I can."

"I want to know the details. All the clinical details."

"That's easy enough. Here, I'll show you the charts."

"I want to know more than that. I want to know where the metal landed. What it did."

"I'll be able to tell you more once I get you under the knife."

"Make notes or something," I said.

When they put the needle in, I relaxed. I looked forward to a sleep without dreams. The dope they had been giving me hadn't been nearly heavy enough. And so the dream came, night after night: Tuyet's happy face, the dispensary open for business, Neumann holding the hand of a child. Ghosts. They whispered to me that it could have been different. And I woke up screaming no.

The stuff they gave me this time was strong. If I saw ghosts, at least I did not remember them. The anesthetic wore off slowly, and I found myself lying on my belly, diapered like a baby. There was not too much pain.

When the doctor finally came around, he brought the fragments with him—ugly black knots of metal. He dropped them into my hand. They were smaller than I had expected them to be. I shook them in my fist like dice as he went on to estimate the velocity at which the shrapnel pierced my flesh, the angle of attack. He correctly guessed that when it had happened I had been prone. That was a safe bet, I suppose. We had learned early to take our hits lying down.

He gave me the placement of the fragments in my body, showing me a bloody little sketch he had made in the operating room. One piece had come within a few millimeters of my bowel. Another had spent its energy and come to rest nestling against a bone.

"That's all I can tell you, Sergeant Morgan," he said. "Any fragments that are still in there will work themselves to the surface in time. There may be a little discomfort, like cutting a tooth, but you're going to be all right."

"Thank you, Doc," I said.

"Every man who comes close," he said, "at least has the right to know just how close he came."

But that wasn't what I was interested in. I wasn't afraid of the metal, or at least no more than I had ever been. In fact, I was depending on it. If I could see the fragments, know exactly what had happened to me and why, then when the ghosts whispered to me that it could have been different, I could prove them wrong.

And later, in the airplane flying home, I was still trying to piece the evidence together. I was going back to the very beginning, seeing how it all added up. I was sitting in the moaning jet and turning the little black knots over and over in my hand. The first thing was why I went at all. They say that in other wars, men went off to battle with visions of glory. I do not know about that. But I do know that we had grown up on different tales. We read stories by men who denied the old lies and understood the new science of necessity, men who did not tolerate abstractions, who knew that all the fancy names people put on their reasons were just a way they had of hiding the brute, animal truth. And in seeking to discover the meaning of these bitter, laconic tales as they applied to our time, we nearly talked the damned thing to death.

Did the medieval monks debate the attributes of the First Cause any more laboriously than we thrashed out the war? For me, the biggest challenge came from a woman I thought I was serious about. And having read the books differently, she believed strongly in right and wrong. As far as she was concerned, it was only proper to fight in self-defense or maybe if the enemy was operating death camps. I suppose we had all been a little spoiled by Hitler.

At some point the debate between Sharon and me shifted. I got my notice for a physical, and the nature of the question was no longer academic. I was scared. I did not know what in hell I was going to be able to do.

"If you don't want to kill," she said, "then don't go."

"It isn't that clear," I said.

"You may have to kill or else die," she said. She was not a person who liked to put things gently.

"Then it might not be so bad."

"You're equivocating."

"Everyone does," I said. "You pay your taxes."

"I do not pay taxes."

"But you're making some money."

"I don't declare it."

"That's not fair."

"In the struggle for liberation," she said, "you have to be shrewd or else you'll be screwed."

When my draft notice came, that pretty much ended the conversation for me. I had to stop talking about it. It only got me more confused. And where I was going, if you hesitated you died.

I tried only once more to explain to Sharon why I was going to let myself be drafted. But I approached it all wrong. I told her that I was sure I wasn't a conscientious objector, citing our mutual response to the invasion of Czechoslovakia. She said that was different. I said I knew she would say that. But I told her that I was neither willing to lie my way out of the draft nor to accept the punishment.

"You aren't confused," she said. "You lack moral courage."

"It's easier for a woman to have moral courage about these things," I said. And that was that. She left me in disgust.

Later I realized that I had not been perfectly honest about it. It probably wouldn't have made any difference to Sharon, but here is how I came to believe I should have explained myself. It wasn't logic, the cold balancing of risks; it wasn't a matter of choice at all. It was something deeper, irresistible. When you came from where I did, when you'd been raised on certain tales, when you'd learned to respect your father and his friends, not because of what they did in the wars but rather because of what they suffered, then you simply had no alternative when your number came up. You were swept along despite the arguments. And it wasn't the great historic ebbs and flows or even the coercive power of the state that did it. You were moved forward by your own ineradicable past. Everything you had ever seen or heard, the whole complex vectoring of forces that had pressed upon you, these were the things that drove you to war. Those unsentimental writers were right. It wasn't duty or honor or country or any lofty imperative. It had nothing to do with courage, moral or otherwise. It was simply who you were.

But that took you only so far and no further. It took me to the army's door. And it left me there. I do not know how to describe the sense of it except to say that I felt utterly abandoned. Even that first day, before I had any real idea of what was ahead except the vague fear of it, I had a premonition that when the shell fragments started winging past and the mortar rounds began to thunder, they would be asking a question, the same damned question: Who are you? Who the hell are you? I hadn't the slightest idea how I would answer. And so when I found Jim Neumann, I suppose it was because in a sense I was looking for him, even though at the very beginning nothing could have seemed more unlikely.

I arrived at Fort Bragg in a cold winter rain. I still remember how strange the place seemed to me as the bus took us from the airstrip to the Reception Center. It was vast and yet confined, wild and yet still highly organized. The only people I saw traveled in step to the drill sergeants' black cadences. There was the smell of the forest in the air, the smell of food cooking.

The Reception Center was a big, drafty barn of a place surrounded by low yellow barracks. The first thing I noticed was the little fence that ran along the walkways and streets. It was made of green shell casings and chain.

Quite a few of us were college graduates. I didn't take a poll or anything. And it wasn't as if anybody was standing around discussing the concept of a just war in Augustine and Aquinas. It was mainly a matter of age. If you were twenty-two, you had escaped to school for a while, not realizing that the war would never end. And if you weren't twenty-two, you were nineteen. There is a big difference in those three years, and I could see it in their faces. Once we went to war, of course, the difference vanished. We all became the same age, older than anyone.

I looked around at my classmates, the hapless graduating class of 1968. Sprawled out on the uncomfortable chairs, they were sullen, physically wrecked. Boozed out. Smoked out. Tapped out. Duds, the drill sergeants would call us. A bunch of duds. Fuck up a two-car funeral. Of course, that wasn't true of all of us. Some of us ended up fighting well. Some even died well, if that still means anything now or ever did. But again, that came later.

From the very start, though, we members of the class of '68 knew enough to keep to ourselves, especially about where we had just been. The beards had all come off before induction. The hair had been chopped back above the collar. It didn't take a college degree to see that as far as the army was concerned you had to be pretty dumb to act smart.

Some of the younger ones were not so quiet. They started to get restless even before our first trip to the mess hall. The soul brothers were the loudest. They were up out of their seats in a state of constant motion, jiving around one tall fellow who sat impassively near the center of the room. This was the Bad Brother. He had an aura of authority so strong I half expected somebody to give him a direct commission. I doubt he had ever met any of the other brothers before that day, but they knew he was the man to reckon with. I do not understand what chemistry it is that makes somebody a natural leader. But the Bad Brother had it. And later I saw that Neumann had it. It was just something you recognized in a man, like intelligence, though it was not the same thing.

"Hey, Sergeant," one of the smaller brothers taunted. "How many of us be going to Vietnam?"

The sergeant did not even look up. He just snorted:

"Every swinging dick."

"These dudes," said another brother, "they think they piss is whiskey just 'cause they been shot at. Why, you got to show something more to prove something to this here dude. A little shootin', hell. No way. It just something that happens. Don't bother this chile."

"Then why you talking 'bout it so?" said the Bad Brother. "You jus' like a junkie jabbering 'bout shit."

It was getting dark outside when they brought the next planeload in from Chicago. Same as us:

old and young, black and white. Huddled together as if that would save them. But there was one among them who stood out from the rest.

He wore a red and white striped jacket that might have been cut from a flag. His hair was long. Several strands of beads dribbled down his front. And on his feet he had some sort of raw leather boots that looked as if he had taken them off an Eskimo. But even if he had not been dressed so peculiarly, he would not have gone unnoticed. He was a head taller than any of the others, broad and hard. And he carried himself with the easy confidence of a natural athlete.

He was at the front of the group when it hit the doorway. He did not pause, blink at the light, the scene of desperation before him. He just strode right in as if it were the most ordinary thing in the world.

"I'm Jim Neumann," he said as he reached the sergeant's desk.

"Lucky you," said the sergeant, paying no attention.

"Did you want to mark it down or something?"

"Sure," said the sergeant to his stack of papers. "Right here in the space where it says jerk-offs."

Then he finally looked up at Neumann, and it might have been Christmas morning.

"Well, well," he said. "We finally got us a hippie. Listen up everybody! They went and drafted us a flower child."

That was not exactly how I would have described Neumann, strange as he looked. I felt sorry for him, being singled out that way, even though he had brought it on himself. But then he said something that surprised me as much as it did the sergeant.

"I wasn't drafted," he said. "I signed up."

"Kid me, hippie," said the sergeant.

"It's right here on the paper."

The sergeant took Neumann's orders and read them, shaking his head.

"Regular Army," he said. "You're a fuckin' RA. I'm an RA, hippie. You know how it makes me feel to know that you're an RA, too?"

Neumann smiled that big, infectious smile he had that made you feel there was nothing that could take him down.

"Lower than whaleshit at the bottom of the ocean," he said.

The sergeant looked at him with eyes that could have wilted any flower.

"If I'm whaleshit, hippie," he said, "what does that make you?"

"I guess it makes me proud to make your acquaintance, brother."

The sergeant tried to hold it back, but he could not. He broke into a stupid grin and handed Neumann back his orders.

"Maybe you'll do OK, hippie, once you take off those funny fuckin' beads."

You have to understand how little I wanted to be hooked up with a character like Neumann at that particular moment. You see, I have always been a great believer in invisibility. When that meant wearing blue blazers, rep ties and button-down shirts, I was a regular little gentleman. Later, when it meant work shirts and jeans, I looked as if I had come straight out of the lettuce fields. You could call this conformism, but I always thought of it more as protective coloration. Now that I was in the army, this principle of camouflage took on even more importance. If they couldn't pick you out of the background, they would have a hard time getting off a clean shot. And so, when the big guy with red beads and a Captain America jacket came bounding across the room, I just hunkered down in my seat.

Naturally, he found me in the crowd. I don't know why, but he came straight toward me, all eyes fastening on him, and sat down in the empty chair on my left.

I acknowledged him, but just barely, and put the gym bag with my shaving kit and books between us. He wasn't carrying anything himself but a small, black, oblong box.

"Been here long?" he said.

"All day," I said. Then I burrowed down in a magazine I had long since exhausted.

"Where from?"

"Chicago."

"No kidding. So am I. You must have been on the first flight."

"First in, first out."

"Feeling short already, are you?" he said. He would not quit. I just nodded my head and pretended to go back to my reading.

"You ever go to the Cumberland Lounge in Chicago?"

"What's that?"

"Cumberland Lounge. It's a club. South Side. Good sounds."

"Can't say as I have."

"Thought I might have recognized you. Thought maybe it was from there. Whereabouts in Chicago do you live?"

"Went to school in Evanston," I said. For some reason I was wary of revealing even my hometown.

"Drafted?"

"Right."

"Well, it's real either way, isn't it?" he said.

That wasn't the kind of question I felt obliged to answer, and so I tried to break the conversation off. This was not easy, though, and not only because Neumann was so persistently friendly. He had a field of force around him, and I was already being drawn into it. Sure, I was abandoned and I was vulnerable. But that doesn't explain away the quality he had. Maybe it was his utter lack of self-consciousness. Maybe it was his enthusiasm. Or maybe I already sensed that he had the instincts that I was afraid I lacked. Whatever it was, it was very strong, even then.

I was the one who finally broke the silence. I came up from out of the magazine and figured it couldn't hurt to talk. He was just sitting there quietly, tapping out a soft, syncopated rhythm on the top of the small black case on his lap.

"You can't carry much in there," I said.

"Everything I need," he said.

"Matched pistols?"

"It's my ax."

"Kind of little for cutting down trees."

"My ax," he said. "My instrument. My horn. Here." He unsnapped the latch and swung open the lid. There, cradled in purple velvet, was a shiny silver flute. He touched his big fingers lightly

35

on the keys, which made small, hollow sounds as they opened and closed.

"Music major," I said. "Maybe they'll put you in the band."

"Don't dig that kind of tune," he said. "I do jazz. The blues. And they don't teach it in school."

"It's a hobby then."

"If life is a hobby," he said.

"Seems like it has been up until now," I said. "College, screwing around. The whole thing. But suddenly it's gotten kind of serious."

"I dropped out of college because I had to get into something real."

"You've done that, all right," I said, directing his attention with my hand to the scene around us. It didn't matter where I pointed. Reality was in every direction.

"I was just wandering. Didn't know what the hell I was doing, where I was going. Read this. Read that. 'The United States in the nineteenth century was marked by a tension between unity and diversity, mobility and stasis. Comment.' I mean, where is that going to get you?"

"Looks like it got you the same place it got me," I said. "Nowhere."

"Here's the thing," he said, closing the case. "When you play the blues, you find out where you're going by going there. You drag something out of yourself, something deep, too deep to get at any other way. Right or wrong, the blues tell you who you are."

Just then the sergeant announced a piss call; his bellowing voice made the opportunity seem like a threat.

"Smoke 'em if you got 'em," he said. "But do it outside. And don't go wandering any farther than my pretty green fences. They're the end of the earth."

Neumann wasn't interested in taking him up on it, but I had to get out of the room. It was beginning to bear down on me, the waiting, the confinement, the sweat end of fear whose stink was getting heavier and heavier.

Outside it was cold and dark, darker than it ever got back in the city. There must have been clouds, because the sky was absolutely black, no stars. A fog was coming in from somewhere. It isolated me all the more.

I lighted a cigarette and moved as far out from the building as the green chains let me go. A wide gravel yard lay in shadows broken only by the lonely light from bare bulbs over doorways. Far away something sputtered like gunfire. I stood there listening to it, the rattle and the punctuating thunder, trying to get a fix on it now while it was still at several removes. The question was only a whisper, but it was going to get louder. I knew it was. I zipped up my jacket against a chill and stamped out the cigarette.

As I started back to the big barn, I heard somebody snap a command. A hundred feet slapped the ground. I looked around, but I could not see for the fog. The feet began to march. The voices began to chant.

> Your left
> Your left
> Your left, right
> LEFT!

They emerged, row by row, from behind a line of barracks. They marched in perfect step. Their shadowy faces were worn. Some limped from hidden wounds. I moved out of their way. But then another cadence struck up. Out of time with the first. Then another. They came from several directions now, closing in on me. I felt trapped, overrun. I grabbed my gym bag under my arm and began to dodge through the gaps in the formations. Shoulders jostled me. Hands shoved me aside. But the movement did not miss a beat. It went on mechanically, as if I were not even there.

Finally, I broke free of them. And when I hit the doorway of the big room, I was dizzy. As I heaved in air and rubbed my eyes to get rid of the spots, I saw something so out of place, so at odds with what had happened outside, that it seemed a vision.

Over in the corner Neumann bent over the thin silver reed, blowing soft blues, simple and melancholy. A bunch of the brothers were gathered around him. The flute was tiny in Neumann's hands, and his shoulders engulfed it.

"Thass right," said one of the brothers. "Thass right."

Neumann was pushing the chords further and further, testing his audience, seeing how far he could carry the men into the abstract added tones high above the song. He played softly, but it filled the room. He swayed like a dancer to the rhythm. He hypnotized.

Then the sergeant broke the spell.

"This ain't no boogaloo parlor," he said. "Fuckin'

lunatics. Don't you guys know? You're all gonna die."

"That's the name of the song," said Neumann as his instrument dropped from his lips.

"We ain't soldiers yet," said the Bad Brother. "We ain't even wearing uniforms. We don't got to take any of this dude's shit."

The other brothers came in behind him, surly and loud.

"He's all right," said Neumann, nodding toward the sergeant. "You got to admit, the Man dug it for quite a few choruses. Not bad for a white dude."

"Shee-it," said the Bad Brother, slapping Neumann's outstretched palm and flashing him a bright, demonic grin.

Neumann and I were eventually assigned to the same platoon. M and N. It was inevitable. We became bunkmates. We became friends.

There wasn't a whole lot of slack time in basic training, so you got to know each other on the run. They woke you up in the dead of night to stand fireguard alone, and you looked out over all the others sleeping in the squad bay and wondered who the hell they were. You mustered out to do push-ups to celebrate the dawn. They pushed you through the mess hall so fast that you didn't have a chance to swallow all your coffee, let alone hold a conversation over it. At night you scrubbed, waxed and buffed the floor, then some damned fool scuffed across it in his boots or knocked over a butt can and you had to do it all over again. When the drill sergeant finally put out the light, it took all the energy you had just to curse him under your breath.

We were stripped down to the essentials, heads shaven, uniforms all the same, no past and damned little in the way of a future. A lot of us even lost our names. Doofus, Professor, Loverboy, anything that was short and sharp was likely to stick with a man. Much later, when I came across a complete list of the casualties and looked for names I knew, I could not tell who had lived and who had died.

And yet you still learned damned near everything of any importance about each other. And it was a knowledge uncluttered by words. You saw some men crumble, some men grow. You saw who was selfish, who was scared. You overlooked most flaws—so long as they did not put you in peril. If a man wanted to be silent, like Neumann, that was all right so long as he was strong. If he was sloppy or ill-kempt, it didn't matter unless we were all punished for his mess. Some guys became isolated in adversity; they were afraid of having to carry any more than their own weight. But others bonded together against it, and the worse it got the closer they became.

I cannot say for sure what it was that made Neumann and me take to one another. We were as different as you could imagine, Neumann fit and decisive, me bookish and hesitant. I suppose in some strange way we compensated for one another: Neumann's instincts and my refined sense of doubt, Neumann's confidence and my reservations, his acts and the explanations I provided for them. But it did not take long before we trusted each other. Within a matter of weeks it was hard to remember that there had ever been a time when I had not known Neumann as a friend.

Our first trainee leader was an eighteen-year-old Georgian who told the drill sergeants he planned to make the army a career. But he did not last long. A small fellow, he made the mistake of thinking power was something somebody gave you, like rank. The brothers ragged him silly, and some of the white guys resented this. The tension grew. Finally, somebody challenged the kid to take off his stripes and fight.

The drill sergeants were delighted. They brought out the heavy gloves, and we circled up inside the bunk line around the squad bay to watch. The Georgian didn't take more than two or three muffled punches before he was on the floor and the sergeants knew he was finished. Then they egged somebody else into the ring, and when he went down, another. It turned into a tournament. Some guys refused to fight, but I put on the gloves and shuffled through a couple of weak opponents until one of the brothers landed one that sat me down. I did not do this for sport, you understand. I did it to show that I was willing to, a matter of credible deterrence.

In the end it came down to Neumann and the Bad Brother. The drill sergeants were putting their money on the Bad Brother because they had seen the way he kept his people in line. Neumann, in contrast, lacked swagger. They knew he was pretty good on the overhead bars and always led the unit on the running track. They knew he handled the pugil stick well enough that he could afford just to hang back and ward off the blows until his opponent tripped himself up and fell. But he did not go on the attack. They thought he lacked aggressiveness, the quality they called the Spirit of the Bayonet. And they probably remembered his beads.

Neumann took off his fatigue blouse to fight in his T-shirt. The Bad Brother stripped down to his big coalhouse chest. I tied Neumann's gloves, had him throw a few jabs into my open palms to get them set.

"Be careful, Jim," I told him. "This guy is tough, and he's got a lot of friends."

After the match got started I felt a little foolish for saying that. The drill sergeants were looking for a successor to the Georgian, the biggest, toughest trainee they could find. I wanted it to be Neumann, not the Bad Brother. I should have told him to knock the sonofabitch's head off.

But Neumann didn't seem to need my coaching. He fended off the first few jabs neatly. He moved. He danced. Not that it was easy. The Bad Brother's reach was nearly as long as Neumann's, and he was quick and strong. When the Bad Brother started to move in on him, Neumann had to throw some hard punches to slow the man down. But the Bad Brother just kept on coming, taking the short, stinging jabs with what looked almost like pleasure.

There were no rounds in this match. The rule was simple: first man to fall. Neither was ahead after five full minutes. Neumann's T-shirt was dark with sweat, and when his left caught the Bad Brother's forehead, the spray came off it like water blown from a breaking wave.

The odd thing was that Neumann never capitalized on the Bad Brother's openings. He had chances, plenty of them. The Bad Brother would fling a roundhouse that failed to connect and find himself all off-balance. Neumann would dance away. The Bad Brother would tire for an instant, let his guard drop. Neumann would wait until he righted himself and bob away from the next frenzy of blows. We screamed for Neumann to deck him. But he did not. The brothers spurred their man on to finish it off. But he could not. The thing went on and on, and the punishment was painful to watch.

Then the Bad Brother seemed to catch a second wind. He flew into Neumann. Blows to the body. Jabs to the head. And then a powerful right, straight off the floor, caught Neumann square. He faltered a moment. The Bad Brother moved in and tried to land another. But to his surprise Neumann parried it and set him back with two sharp jabs.

That was when it ended, and not by the drill sergeants' rules. The two of them were in a clinch, chests heaving against one another. Neumann pushed the Bad Brother away and brought his hands up on the defense again. But the Bad Brother stepped back away from him, put out his own hands and waved the fight to a halt.

"You took . . . all I . . . I could give you," he breathed. "I'll go on . . . if you want. . . . But you took the best."

The other brothers let out a howl. Some of the white guys wanted it settled once and for all, too. But the two fighters weren't hearing any of it.

"I call it even," said Neumann as he moved toward the Bad Brother and grabbed a gloved hand awkwardly between his own.

"For a white man, hippie," said the Bad Brother, "you ain't so bad your own self. . . . Where'd you learn to dance like that?"

"If you have to learn it," Neumann said, "you're never going to know."

"Like the blues," said the Bad Brother.

"There you go, my friend. . . . There you go."

The drill sergeants had to wait until the company commander returned from a weekend away before they named Neumann trainee leader. It was one of those decisions they had to make the officer think was his own. But they let Neumann in on the plan as soon as the crowd broke up.

Later we sat on our footlockers as he toweled the sweat off and got into dry clothes. He was acting strange for a winner, kind of irritable. I figured that maybe the adrenaline was still pumping and that it was better to leave him alone. But when I made a move to stand up, he stopped me.

"Is that the way it's going to be now?" he said. "You're just going to walk away?"

"Any way you want it," I said.

"These fatigues are shot," he said, wadding them up and stuffing them into the laundry bag tied to the post of the bunk. "I broke starch this morning. Now they look like I wore them to bed."

"Nobody will notice the wrinkles Monday," I said. "They'll all be looking at those stripes."

He did not seem amused. It was as if there was something in particular he wanted me to say. I had no idea what it was, but I tried anyway.

"You fought a hell of a fight, Jim. You could have decked him if you had wanted."

"I guess." He folded down the leather tops of

his boots, tucked his pants legs into them just so, then laced them up.

"I kind of figured they'd give the winner the promotion," I said. "Survival of the fittest. You wanted it, didn't you?"

"Look," he said, "the sergeants say they're going to give us a treat tonight. They set up some kind of movie in one of the classrooms down the road. Maybe we can break away."

"Go AWOL?"

"That against your principles?"

It just seemed odd to me that he wanted to flout authority at the very moment that he got a piece of it for himself.

"No," I said. "Hell no."

"I can never be sure," he said. "You seem to have so many of them."

As it turned out, my problem wasn't principles. It was fear. As the company queued up at the door of the classroom building I felt Neumann's hand grab at my elbow and yank me around a corner into the shadows. We waited there until all of them were inside. Then Neumann reconnoitered to see that none of the sergeants were lying in wait. When he was sure, he signaled to me and we made a break. There was nothing to it, really, except trying to keep from thinking what would happen to us if we got caught.

The way Neumann had it figured, we had at least two hours before anybody would miss us. We moved carefully through the training center, behind barracks, in the darkness between mess halls. It felt strange, being on our own for once, nobody telling us where to go, when to double-time, when

45

to halt. More than once we spotted an officer or sergeant, and we had to lie back until the danger passed.

When we finally reached the main highway, we hid in the bushes until a car came along that did not have a lifer in it—you could tell by the official bumper sticker when it was somebody you were supposed to salute or obey—then we hitched a ride. The man driving was some kind of tradesman. He acted as if he knew what we were up to. In fact, he offered to take us to the main enlisted men's club.

"Don't worry none," he said. "That's where the trainees go on graduation week. Nobody'll know the difference."

I acted as if I did not know what he was talking about. It was as if Neumann and I were operating deep behind enemy lines. You couldn't be too careful. But the man just laughed at my efforts.

He let us off at the door of a big frame building and told us the quickest way back in case we had to go on foot. He asked us what training company we were with, and I lied. Neumann did not correct me, but he shook the man's hand and said, "Seems like you've been through this before."

"Once in a while," the man said. "Even a fuckin' trainee sometimes has a pair of balls. If you don't go sneakin' off once in a while, you ain't got the makin's of a soldier, far as I'm concerned."

"Thanks," said Neumann, as I pulled him away.

Already I wanted to turn around and beat a retreat. But I knew Neumann wouldn't be satisfied with that, so I figured we could just have a couple of beers, call it a great adventure, then get the hell back to the barracks before they turned out the lights. I was a little nervous walking into the joint. I didn't know what to expect. The club was dark and loud with soul music. A strange mirrored ball hung from the ceiling as though it were from some Depression musical, and spots flashed spiraling on the walls.

The place was full of skinhead trainees trying to get themselves drunk. There were even a few women, but they all seemed to belong to somebody. The bartender didn't even look at us as he drew us two glasses of weak beer.

"Jesus, is that fine," I said, sipping mine. "You forget after a while what it's like to be alive."

"The man in the truck was right. If you're going to be a soldier, you've got to go it alone sometimes."

And suddenly it dawned on me why Neumann wanted to be trainee leader and why he wanted to go AWOL once he got it.

"That's why you wanted the promotion," I said, "to get leverage. You thought it was a way to get some control over what happens to us."

Neumann turned toward me and smiled. I had finally gotten it right.

"But why didn't you take the Bad Brother down? You could have. I know you could have."

"It was what you said before the fight," he said. "You said the Bad Brother had a lot of friends."

"It was a stupid thing to say."

"No," said Neumann. "You were right. I knew I was going to have to live with the man. I didn't want to humiliate him. A man needs to have his pride."

"You're still going to have your hands full," I said.

"We're all going to," said Neumann. "You've got to be ready when you go across the pond."

"What's Vietnam like in June?" I said.

"Why June?"

"That's when I figure we might be getting there," I said. "Of course, you can't be sure. Anything could happen. They could send us to Germany. They could train us to operate in arctic conditions. We could get sick, if we're lucky, and put it off for a while. Maybe the war will end."

"We should live so long," he said.

"Nicely put," I said. "Bring this man another beer."

But I wasn't really thinking about dying. The danger I was afraid of was more immediate. I still had my eye on the door in case one of the sergeants should come in looking for us.

"When we get across the pond," he said, "I want us to know what to do and what not to. To have some say over it."

"Speak for yourself," I said, holding up my hand. "Look at those highly trained typist's fingers. I plan to be somebody's loyal, safe company clerk."

"Better not count on it," he said. "I've been thinking about NCO school. We're going to volunteer for it. Earn a few permanent stripes."

"This near beer has gone to your head," I said.

"It would give us leverage."

"Responsibility," I said. "Stripes are for lifers, Jim. Stripes just give the bad guys something to aim at."

Neumann was silent as the bartender brought

us another round. I sipped the beer and pretended it still tasted good. I was sorry Neumann had brought it up, because I knew that once he got an idea like this in his head he would not give it up lightly. Worse, he would not be satisfied until he persuaded me to go along with it, too. Whether it was going AWOL or volunteering to lead men in battle, he always seemed to want my approval.

"You think about it, Morgan," he said. "Here's the thing: You want to get into a position where you can call some of the shots."

"It isn't a game of pool," I said, and we left it at that.

We got back to the barracks safely that night and slipped into the squad bay while everybody was playing grab-ass and talking about how much cleavage Raquel Welch had shown. Nobody even noticed the smell on our breath.

On Monday the CO made the announcement about Neumann, and even the brothers seemed to accept it. Everybody could see that he had the kind of universal competence that, perhaps just because it is so uncommon, people like to call common sense.

From then on we trained to Neumann's count. We hiked. We ran. We did push-ups and side-straddle hops. I'm not saying it was easy, even with Neumann leading us. At first the tempo always seemed wrong. On long marches our natural strides caused the whole line to string out like an accordion. Then the sergeant would scream, "Tighten up!" And if you were at the back of the line, you had to race like hell to catch up. It wore you out. After a while, though, the problem went away. Our paces became indistinguishable. Our files stayed tight. No more running. We walked as one. It was so much easier. It was inhuman.

We learned about the Spirit of the Bayonet. It was "TO KILL!" They made us scream the words back at them, a devil's catechism. At first I tried to find something else to yell: "BLUE GILL!" or "TO BALL!" But as time passed, that just seemed silly. "TO KILL!" echoed off the barracks as we chanted it, all of us. And it came back as a reminder of just how far we had gone.

But Neumann always reached the objective way ahead of us. And he was impatient with anyone who lagged behind. Whenever one of the weak sisters fell out during a march or collapsed in the middle of physical training, Neumann hauled him up by the shoulders and got him moving again. He would not listen to any talk of pain. He had no tolerance for the tortured moral excuses and sullen complaints that came from the mouths of the college grads and streetwise blacks. I saw him force men to go beyond the limits of their endurance, to transcend their weaknesses and qualms the way his blues music transcended the limitations of the chords. He showed us how to overcome the obstacles, how to trick courage out of our doubts, how to survive.

Some men were broken when they could not do what he demanded. They checked into the infirmary with exhaustion; they wept quietly in their bunks at night. Some were mustered out of service as unfit. Others were held back for another session of training. Those of us who made it saw nothing wrong with this. These men were simply not ready, and it was better for them and for us that they failed in training rather than later when lives were at stake. Maybe we sometimes felt sorry for the duds, the humiliation the drill sergeants put them through, the utter collapse of their pride. But they got no pity from Neumann. He was too busy preparing us all for war. And, I think, he simply refused to accept that there was anything that would not shape itself to the will. The harder the challenge, the more exhilarated he became; the more difficult the changes, the more they ignited his improvisations.

But what was will to him was sheer necessity to the rest of us. And each man found a personal way of bending to it. My way was to detach myself from the whole business, to think of it as watching somebody else. I split in two. Somebody else was crawling through the mud, shining his belt buckle every night and caring about how well it reflected. Somebody else was grunting in an open line of toilets with five other guys, polishing the floor inch by inch with a facecloth. Somebody else submitted, not me. I was just watching Morgan's progress.

It felt a lot better that way, just to be watching. What did it matter if they tear-gassed Morgan, forced him to crawl under machine-gun fire? No sweat. Morgan just did what he was told.

But when it came to mortality, there was no holding back. The two became one again. You couldn't get any distance from death. I remember especially the day they trained us on the M-16.

"It's gonna be your best friend, men," said the drill sergeant, and you didn't know whether he was borrowing from the movies or the other way around. "It's a little fucker, but it's mean as can be."

We had been using the long, heavy M-14 for six weeks. Compared with it, the M-16 felt like a Mattel toy. It was lightweight. It hardly kicked at all. I joked about it until I put it on automatic and fired off a full clip before I could even think to stop. They assured us that if an M-16 round struck an enemy soldier anywhere, that was the end of the game. As soon as the round hit, they said, it began to tumble end over end.

"It ain't exactly a dumdum," said the drill sergeant, "but it's just as good. All perfectly legal, you understand. So legal that Charlie uses them too. An AK-forty-seven works just exactly like a good old American M-sixteen, and Charlie can get you just as easy as you can get him. Uncle Sugar tries to stay ahead of the game, men. He really does."

The longer training went on, the more you had to confront just what it was they were training you for. You could grumble about the wet, endless days on the rifle range, but when the target popped up, it had the silhouette of a man. You could bitch about the way they made you crawl up and down the piny dunes, but you had to admit that it made sense to keep your profile low. You did not even try to kid yourself about what you might be facing. You sought it out. You grilled the drill sergeants about their experiences in the jungles across the pond. You tried to get a perfect fix on all the dangers.

"They got snakes over there?"

"Ol' Jake?" the drill sergeant said. "Jake No-Shoulders? Got to watch out for Jake the Snake all the time. Kill you faster than a motherfucker."

"Gaw-aw-aw-awd damn," said the guy who swore like an ignition trying in vain. "They have tigers, too?"

"Tigers, elephants," said the sergeant, "the whole motherfuckin' circus. And we supply the clowns."

Animals or men, wise guys or fools, the game was the same. It was a mortal fight, and only those who were fit for it would survive. But if that was the meaning of combat—brute nature and the odds—then courage, loyalty, moral choice and blame were only words. We were in the army, the Green Machine, and we were heading for the green, primal jungles. Between the two of them, there was nothing for a soldier to decide. He only did what he had to do.

Neumann, of course, did not believe in this, at least before Xuan The. He resisted the odds, denied necessity. He accepted responsibility for every damned thing he did. Neumann's way was the blues, the tones and sequences he dragged out from within himself, the cadences of his own heart.

At times I wanted to see it Neumann's way. But there was something seductive about surrendering to forces outside your control, beyond choice or blame. After all, I did not choose the methods of killing I was learning. I would have preferred not to fire at the silhouette's shoulders, to jab my bayonet into the dummy's rubber breast. And yet

I wanted to master these techniques now, for they were the tools of survival. I wanted to be able to use them when I needed to, and only then. But if you surrendered, how could you be sure you wouldn't go too far? This was the knot: Either there was nothing you could do about it or else there wasn't anything you might not do. Green or blue. That was the personal problem.

Finally, our orders came. An omniscient computer somewhere in the Green Machine spat them out. It tumbled through punch cards as if it were dealing from a deck. Neumann and I drew the same hand: Eleven Bravo, light weapons infantrymen.

Neumann was absolutely exuberant about it. He understood that the rest of us were less pleased, so he tried not to act like the guy who won the sweepstakes. But I could tell from the way he moved from man to man in the squad bay, congratulating the clerks and bucking up the other Eleven Bushes, that he had gotten exactly what he wanted.

It was a Saturday. We had the rest of the day to ourselves. The drill sergeants passed among us offering to buy whiskey. Neumann had something else in mind. He came over to my bunk and told me we were going for a hike in the country. I told him I was a city boy.

But then he pulled out an old, beaten-up Marlboro box. There were at least five rolled joints inside it. Still, I hesitated.

"To the woods," he said.

You hate to let a friend down.

We filled canteens with Kool-Aid, bought some hamburgers at the PX and set out toward the hills.

Neumann seemed to know exactly where he was going. He led me miles from the barracks to a small saddle between two rises. Below us spread a wide, grassy meadow. The ground where we finally came to rest bore a soft cover of pine needles. Our hollow lay in the early afternoon sun and sheltered us from the wind. We relaxed awhile, letting the sun evaporate the sweat from our fatigues.

Neumann tapped me on the knee and pointed to the meadow. He motioned for me to stay put and keep quiet. A full-grown doe grazed peacefully below us. I watched Neumann move softly and surely down the slope, tacking from tree to tree to keep his face into the breeze and conceal his movements. I lost him in a treeline and then saw him emerge again not fifty yards from the deer. He crouched behind some bushes and watched the animal as it ate. Then he started back up the hill as carefully as he had gone down. The deer never caught his scent. It finally moved slowly out of the meadow into the trees.

Neumann returned beaming.

"Did she ever sense me?"

"She ate her fill, then she walked away."

He lighted a joint, sucked smoke and, with a self-satisfied expression, handed it over to me. I took my turn, the dope icy in my throat.

"Good weed," I said. "Makes everything seem just fine."

"No," he said lazily. "You have to do that for yourself. Dope is what you make of it, just like anything else."

I was too mellow to argue with him, so I just

took the joint back when he handed it to me and had a deep, deep pull.

The grass was strong, and so we both giggled. The burgers tasted awfully fine when we finally ate them. The Kool-Aid was as sweet as life itself. The birds sang, and Neumann took out his silver flute and answered them. He may have been playing poorly for all I know.

"You stalked that deer like you knew what you were doing," I said when he had finished his song.

"Used to hunt," he said. "Montana. Then I stopped."

"Moved East?"

"Heard a story."

"Well, tell it, for Christsake. Tell it."

He leaned back into the needles, stretched his legs and put his hands behind his head.

"A certain hunter had been out for grizzly for three days in the mountains when he finally got the trail of one," he said. "He stalked it from morning till night. The going was hard, but he kept at it, and every step he took through the rocks and forests made getting the bear more and more important to him. He had never had such a clever quarry before, and his pride drove him on beyond exhaustion. Finally, he spotted the bear in full view in a scraggly clearing.

"The way the story goes, the hunter's aim went bad because he paid his aim too much mind. He hit the bear, but he didn't drop it. It crashed off into the bush, and when the hunter got down to the clearing he could see by the blood that he had wounded it pretty badly. Dusk was on him, so he made camp to get rested for the final stalk in the morning.

"The hunter got crazy drunk that night. It was the satisfaction that intoxicated him as much as the whiskey. He finally passed out and dreamed of the bear's ugly head above his fireplace, teeth bared in the final disgrace and subjugation.

"But the bear hadn't run far. It was wounded badly and dying fast. It seemed to know it. When night fell, it turned back in its tracks. It found the hunter asleep and it attacked. In a daze, the hunter managed to get his rifle. He killed the bear with a shot under the jaw, but not before the bear had torn him up badly.

"The hunter crawled his way to a road somehow. He told the story to the people who picked him up. He insisted on telling it, even though he was weak and bleeding. He died before they got him to a hospital."

Neumann turned toward me. The dope had put up a screen between us, but something was projected there. His face changed as if in a slow-motion film. The furrows in his forehead smoothed out like a sheet on a bunk under your palm. The corners of his mouth turned up and he showed his teeth. I saw the pride of the hunter and the snarl of the bear. I saw that there was more to his instincts than just the instrumental ways of survival. You not only had to know how to kill, you had to know when and why, or else you were going to destroy yourself, too.

"I don't know how I'll ever be able to pull the trigger on another man," I said.

Neumann, smiling now, began to laugh.

"You will," he said. "You will."

And I could not keep myself from laughing, too, because in those words Neumann had captured both the future tense and the present, both fate and choice.

"The green and the blue," I said.

It seemed unbelievably funny stoned.

# 2
# Green

After we got our orders as infantrymen, I was full of doubts. But not about where we were going to go from there. We were on the Green Machine, barreling toward Vietnam, and it was only a matter of time.

But it was a long way across the pond, and after basic training we were not even close. We had plenty of time to think about what was coming. Plenty of time to brood. The first stop was Advanced Infantry Training, and that was where they began to separate the grunts from all other forms of animal life.

It was about midway through AIT that I finally let Neumann persuade me to go on to NCO school with him. It wasn't that I had gotten sure of myself. I had come to depend on Neumann even more. I did not want to go it alone.

At the end of the course, when they proclaimed us shake-and-bake buck sergeants, they said we were ready to lead men in battle. As long as I was around Neumann, I half-believed it about being ready.

After taking our accumulated leave time, we shipped out of Fort Dix together on a brisk fall morning, dressed for the tropics. We flew by way of Anchorage, and it was like going through all the seasons in the course of a day, because when we finally touched down at Bien Hoa at midnight and they opened the door of the cabin, it was a summer like no summer I had ever known. The air rushed in like poison, hot and choking. I caught a whiff of the jungles, something dead there. I was not prepared for the heat and smell. I was not ready at all.

A tall, self-important Spec-4 with a drooping moustache told us how to find the bunkers in case of attack. Then he led us behind the terminal to where our duffel bags lay in piles. The only light came from the terminal itself, which was nothing more than a wide, flat roof supported by timber beams over a dirty floor and some benches. Outside in the dim, angling light, moths cast the shadows of eagles. They fluttered over us as we found our bags and dragged them to the bus.

Once we got on board we were silent. It was dark. We were exhausted and scared. We did not know where we were. The soft rattle of the engine and the scuff of feet were lost in a cavernous hush. Then the bus heaved up the narrow road. It drove past piles of supplies and long rows of vehicles. At the airport gate an armored car with a machine gun mounted on top pulled in front of us. The gunner held his weapon parallel to the ground and scanned the street.

I glanced at Neumann. He sat with his arms crossed over his chest. His eyes were closed. I wanted to ask him something, ask him anything. But the silence in the bus was too deep to interrupt. I eased slowly down in my seat.

The buildings along the road—dark, looming forms—curved in on us like the walls of a cave. Here and there a point of light shone out from between louvers. Warm, flickering light. The bright points made constellations on the dark horizon of the street. But they were not ones we knew. You could not take your bearings on them; they only told us how hopelessly we were lost.

Then the town was gone, and the horizon opened wide across flat fields. The bus picked up speed. The armored car swung in a wide U-turn on a concrete, four-lane road rimmed with barbed wire high as a house. The bus pulled into a gate marked 90th Replacement Battalion.

I did not get much sleep that night. My chest was too tight, my mind too loose. When a breeze did come, it was a ghost whispering. I expected to hear our guns firing. Where the hell were the guns? It was too easy to imagine death in the silence.

When the sun came up, instead of the vision of desolation I had expected, a vast and crowded compound stretched before me. The sun had exploded on the horizon, bright red and parching. The shadows it cast were as sharp as a razor. In every direction there were barracks, mess halls, jeeps and deuce and a halfs, GIs wandering around unarmed. I smelled bacon cooking. And pretty soon there was another smell. It turned out to be shit on fire.

It seemed that the water table was so high that the only safe sewage system was the flame. And so a hapless detail was formed to drag the buckets from under the latrines, douse them with oil and light them up. The smoke blew our way as we waited in the chow line. Later, much later, I came to welcome this smell. As they said in the bush, you knew you weren't in deep shit if you were close enough to smell it burning.

A short distance away from the mess hall the mama-sans were filing into camp. Some dressed in silken pajamas, wide hats made of cane. Others wore pieces of our uniforms, T-shirts, caps, olive-drab pants. Each in turn had to raise her arms and suffer a body search administered by a burly MP. He patted down their hips, between their legs, up their chests.

I was just beginning to feel sorry for them and ashamed of our behavior when the first explosion hit. It thundered off the buildings, echoed on down the line. I had no idea where it came from. Somebody yelled, "Incoming!" I hit the ground and covered my head with my hands.

Then I felt someone tugging at me. I looked up. It was Neumann, pulling me to my feet.

"The bunkers," he said. "They've got bunkers."

Another explosion ripped past us as we ran to a pathetic little culvert covered over with sandbags. I dove into it and huddled down on my knees. I suppose I might even have prayed.

Two more blasts shook the earth, and I was sure

that at any moment one of the mama-sans would appear in the opening with a rifle or a satchel charge to finish us off. But all I saw was the sun and the dust. The sirens began to wail.

Neumann was first to stick his head out. I stayed hunkered against the cool, wet soil.

"It's all clear," Neumann shouted in at me as the explosions grew more muffled. "That's just outgoing."

But I was no hero. Neumann's shadow moved away and I waited, gazing out at the emptiness. Then, finally, I began to inch my way back onto the face of the earth. I was amazed at what I saw.

The base camp was going on with business as usual, a great reclining beast stung by flies. You couldn't even see where the rounds had landed. Somebody who had been in country awhile explained that the rockets were big but they weren't really so bad. They were pretty much like lightning striking, he said, because Luke the Gook set them crudely, floating a bobber in a bucket so that it detonated when the water evaporated and Luke was long gone. They could not really aim them, he said, not like the mortars. Mortars meant somebody was out there bracketing in on you.

But I was beyond reassurance. The sheer randomness appalled me. Nobody even seemed to know whether anyone had been killed. Neumann tried to drag me back to the chow line, but I had lost my appetite.

"It's going to be bad," I said.

"You'll make it," he said.

"I feel stuck, Jim. I don't know what I'm going to do."

He took off his steel-pot and ran his fingers around the brim, bright camouflage-green, fresh from the box.

"You're going to have to move," he said. "Just loosen up and move."

"It's easy for you," I said. "You have something inside that tells you what to do. But I don't have the instincts, Jim. And when they start lobbing in the shells, you can't sit down and figure out the trajectory."

He held his helmet at arm's length in front of him. The sour smoke from one of the fires wafted over us.

"Watch," he said as he let go. The helmet tumbled to the ground. "See. It's no different from anyplace else."

The clouds rolled in at noon that day, and we were in for a spell of light rain and mortars. The rain was a constant drizzle touched with lightning. The mortars came in clusters of two or three.

Somebody blamed the attacks on the Paris peace talks. Somebody else said the bad guys were cranking up for an offensive. There was some discussion about whether the lifers had set up the barrages as a kind of training exercise for us. Then the rumor went around that several people had actually been killed. But we all agreed that the deaths did not prove a thing, lifers being what they were.

When we fell in the next morning, they had heaps of equipment and stacks of rifles waiting for us. Issued: one flak jacket, one pistol belt, six clips, one M-16. They wrote down the serial numbers of the rifles behind our names on a roster.

"All this shit's yours but the weapons and ammo, men," said the first sergeant. "They're mine. You're getting them just for the day because you have a little business to attend to. When you finish I want the sixteens back. Thems of you that gets greased, you'll be excused from further obligation."

Then he told us to stand at ease and light up if we wanted. We were about to have a special opportunity, the first shirt said On-the-job training, a little good OJT.

"Colonel's got a case of the ass about the mortars, men," said the first shirt. "Wants something done. He got this hunch about where they might be set up. And so he thinks to himself, all I need is some men to chase them out. And, by God, it dawns on him. The one thing he's got is men. Got 'em coming out the ass. A little green, maybe, but so is everything else that comes out the ass in this fucked-up place.

"In short, men, you been volunteered."

A complaint shuddered through the ranks. It wasn't fair. We were too new for this sort of thing, or too short. We were too young to die. Or too old. Both.

One man, though, was not displeased. A ruddy guy in the last file let out a loud, triumphant whoop. Even the first sergeant looked at him funny when he did it.

Then the lieutenant got up and started off by making a patriotic speech, which was not encouraging. His plan was to leave by the front gate, walk down the highway to a small dirt road, then off to the northeast where a group of little villages hunched up against the jungles. Trinh An One,

Three and Four were the villages' names. Nobody knew what had happened to Trinh An Two. And we were so new that some of us worried about it.

The first shirt gave us ten minutes before saddling up. I leaned against a hootch and pulled out the knife I had bought back at Abercrombie & Fitch on my last leave at home. It was long and shiny, and it had a mottled horn grip. I felt the point, drawing blood at the tip of my finger. Then I rubbed the blade against my fatigue pants to give the edge a last fine honing. I had bought it because I figured it would be good for odd jobs like cutting rope and scraping off caked mud. But these were not the only reasons. It had caught my eye in the store window because of the cleanliness of line and material. And though I hated to admit it, when I picked it up and wielded it in my palm, when I imagined it biting into flesh, I liked the shape it gave my hand.

"Nice shiv."

I looked up. It was the guy who had let out the war whoop. His name tag said Thompson. And his expression said he was definitely hard-core.

"Pretty fancy," he said. "How much you take for it?"

"Think I'll just keep it."

"What'd it cost you?"

"Don't remember."

"Give you twenty," he said. "Thirty."

"I don't think so, thanks."

"Good for gutting dinks," he said.

I put the knife back in its scabbard on my pistol belt and snapped the leather thong shut around its handle.

"Might could get a chance to use it this morning," he said. He leered at me, poked an imaginary blade into my belly and gave it a sharp twist. Then he winked and walked away.

I joined Neumann and waited for the order to fall in. Near us an overweight little guy whose fatigues were too long and too tight struggled to get his pistol belt sized around his gut. His bloated fingers fumbled with the hooks and elusive eyes. Finally, the whole mess thumped to the ground.

"Let me give you a hand with that," Neumann said. He loosened the web belt and put it around the little man's waist, cinching it there just above where his hips should have been. It sagged but held.

"It'll stay there better when they issue the suspenders," Neumann said.

"I'm a clerk," said the fat man. "I'm supposed to be a clerk."

"Relax," said Neumann.

Rain ran down the fat man's face. Hollows grew in his cheeks and sank his eyes, fear overcoming flesh.

"My brother was here," he said. "He told me about these villages. They may look peaceful. People will bow, children smile. But they'll blow you away in a minute if you give them a chance.

"My brother said the VC are always watching. They see through the eyes of the little kids peering from doorways, the old ladies doing their wash. You can feel the blade against your throat as you pass a young girl slicing fruit."

"He must be some storyteller," said Neumann.

"They weren't just stories. He told us all about it in his letters. Then he was killed."

In a way that I did not appreciate at the time, nor even now fully understand, I recognized for just an instant a hint of what would happen to us in Xuan The. And sometimes I wonder whether it wasn't our expectation of deceit more than deceit itself that proved so corrupting.

The first shirt called us together and we moved out. The company clerk, permanently stationed in Long Binh, humped the radio. He was a Polish kid the first shirt naturally called Ski, and he seemed even more nervous than the rest of us. I asked him whether he knew of the villages.

"Roger that," he said.

"Bad?"

"The pits," he said.

We moved past the last wire and onto the highway in the dark. It was deserted, and the rain tapped on the concrete. At some point the lieutenant pulled out his plastic laminated map, spun it around a couple times as he tried to orient it to the dark terrain. Then he finally gave up and led us off down a dirt road.

"Dead reckoning," Neumann said. He thought it was funny.

Ski's nerves were getting more animated. Thompson twitched with anticipation. Neumann began to stalk, hands up and ready, muscles poised.

Then we came in sight of the ville. It sort of hung there before us in the blue shadows, desolate and empty. The lieutenant ordered us to move out slowly on line.

We inched up toward the hootches, spread out

across a field. Any moment I expected to be cut off at the knees. Every tuft of grass I stepped on triggered a mine in my mind. A dog barked and six men went to their bellies.

It wasn't until we got very close that the sign flashed in front of us.

First it flickered, and we ducked. Then it lighted up full, and a little chuckle crackled through the line like fire.

MAJIC FINGERS MASSAGE, the sign said.

In the next hootch over, a door opened up. A bent old man came out, saw us, then ran back into his shack. He emerged a moment later with an armload of cans.

"Beer here," he said.

The lieutenant sharply rebuked two of the men who broke ranks and raced for the refreshments.

"Keep it orderly," the lieutenant said. And so, like gentlemen, we queued up to wait our turn.

The fat man seemed calmer now, though he did not risk their beer. Thompson was visibly disappointed. And Ski still fidgeted. I couldn't understand why until the door of the Majic Fingers opened up and somebody inside let out a cry. Half the unit went for their rifles. The other half laughed. Out came a pretty Vietnamese girl about eight months gone. On her tiny frame the baby she bore was enormous. She had to lean backward to balance it as she walked toward Ski.

"You come home," she said.

"Oh, shit," said Ski, and from then on the scene was quite domestic.

We stuck around the ville for a while. There were no mortars, at least none we could find. The rain let up. Ski and his girl discussed the uncertainties of paternity and then retired to the hootch. By the time I finished my beer, I had forgotten about the fat man's warning. When it didn't kill you, Vietnam could be a farce. And that was one of its ways of leading you into the trap.

Meanwhile, Neumann had taken an interest in a group of village children. He borrowed my knife, and the kids crowded around him as he demonstrated the progressively more difficult tricks of mumblety-peg. When he flipped it off his nose, they laughed. When he snapped it off the back of his hand, they jumped up and down in purest admiration. Thompson was admiring it, too. He tried once again to buy the knife, but Neumann told him he would have to see me about it.

When the first shirt finally told us to saddle up, Neumann hung back. He had one more trick. He cleared the kids out from behind him, glanced over his shoulder and deftly flipped the blade in a high, backward arch. It sailed up over his head and, the point dropping down gracefully, headed for the dirt. Thompson's hand darted out to grab it. But he only got a piece of the grip, and the knife went flying into the middle of the crowd of boys. Somebody screamed.

Neumann pushed his way among them.

"Is anybody hurt?" he yelled.

The children fell silent but for one tiny voice weeping. Neumann bent down.

"Medic!" he yelled.

But by the time the medic got there, the weeping had stopped. Neumann led a small, dark, half-breed boy out of the crowd, and the boy proudly presented for bandaging a tiny cut on his arm.

We finally got organized and moved out back toward Long Binh. The boys and girls all waved and said, "OK. OK. OK." The women waved, too. Ski came running out of the hootch, a little disheveled, buckling his pants. And some of the men in the unit vowed bravely, like MacArthur, to return.

When we got back to the compound, we turned in our rifles, stowed the rest of our gear in our footlockers and went off to the mess hall. I listened to the lies we were telling each other for a while, then I got tired of them and returned to the hootch.

It seemed empty, but when I reached the top of the stairs I noticed somebody crouching near my footlocker. I couldn't see him clearly. He kneeled with his back toward me, and the line of the bunks obscured him. I came up on him quietly. It was Thompson.

"What's up?" I said, as nicely as I could.

He stood and turned.

"You left your footlocker open," he said. "I was closing it for you."

"It was already closed."

He circled away as I moved closer.

"You saying I been stealing?"

"I'm not saying anything except don't be messing with my stuff. Just get out of here."

"I don't steal from nobody."

"Well, you better not steal from me, Thompson, or I'll throw your ass into a hurt."

"Piece of shit," he said as he backed off to the stairway.

I opened the locker. The knife was still there. It lay on top of the dark, unfaded tropical fatigues they had issued us. I picked it up and ran the blade up my forearm. It nipped off hair and flakes of skin.

I had been living in the same fatigues since we left Fort Dix, and they were wet and foul. I stripped off my socks and pulled on clean ones. The new fatigues were so fresh they smelled like a store. I looked for one of those olive-drab handkerchiefs they issued and found it deep in the corner. I barely heard the scraping of footsteps on the stairs.

Then I felt a vague sense of someone behind me and I turned on my knee. Thompson was coming toward me behind the pick end of an entrenching tool.

"Nobody calls me a thief, motherfuck," he said.

I managed to get up and move backward. My body tensed and my hands came up for protection.

"You stoned?" I asked. "Drunk?"

"Boy, I'm gonna hurt you real bad or either I may jes' kill you."

"Easy, Thompson," I said.

"Don't nobody call me a thief."

"Take it easy. I don't say you're a thief. Let's let it pass. No harm done. Just take it easy."

"Don't nobody never call me no thief."

I was backing off slowly as Thompson advanced. The point of the entrenching tool bobbed back and forth toward the place where my neck met my shoulders. I talked too fast. I tried to tell him I wouldn't say anything about it if he would just go away. But he wasn't listening. I moved to the center aisle between the bunks and started circling. He watched me sweat as I looked for the motion that would signal his attack. I circled into a pillar and knocked down a butt can. The water on the floor made me slip. He darted forward, made a half-swing. I swerved aside and started circling again.

Then a change came over Thompson's face. I jumped back. The pick didn't fall.

"Ain't got nothin' to do with you," Thompson said. I turned my head slightly. Neumann stood at the top of the stairs. He moved up next to me.

"Put it down," he said.

"Get back. Ain't got nothin' to do with you." He menaced Neumann with the point of the tool.

"I don't want any part of that thing," Neumann said. "Just put it down and then we'll . . ."

Neumann's driving shoulder pinned him hard to the floor. The tool flew toward me and crashed against a pillar. I got it and tossed it out of reach.

Thompson gasped for breath and tried to wrench away. Neumann shifted a little to let him breathe, but Thompson got a hand free and clawed for Neumann's face. When the fist finally hit Thompson's mouth, it whipped his head around and threw it back against the linoleum. He was out cold.

"Get the first sergeant," Neumann said. "I'll try to bring him to."

Even before I got down the stairs I started to worry about it. Maybe he wasn't trying to steal the knife. Maybe he was just locking my locker like he said. Maybe I'd forgotten to lock it after all. The only thing certain was Thompson's head on the warped green linoleum, thrown back awkwardly into a puddle of stale water, a drool of blood slipping from his lips to the floor.

"Just remember one thing," Neumann said later.

"I know," I said. "He might have killed me with the tool. But maybe it didn't need to happen at all. Maybe I was wrong about Thompson. . . ."

"Maybe. Maybe. Maybe," Neumann said.

"Up and out of the fartsacks," the first shirt shouted in the dark. "Crawl offa them cum pads. You're going off to war."

We were already seasoned enough that we could laugh about it as we climbed into our fatigues and got ready for what we expected to be another morning formation devoted to helpful information about oral hygiene and the clap. But this time it turned out the first shirt wasn't kidding. When we formed up in the sandy square, he started reading off names. Thompson got some kind of dangerous duty he had volunteered for. Neumann was on the list for the 82nd Airborne. I drew orders for the 1st Cavalry Division, and it seemed as though we were scattering to the far ends of the universe.

Neumann and I shook hands, promising to stay in touch. "Keep your head down," he said and slapped my back. And that was that.

Even though I had always known that someday

it would happen, I was not ready to be separated from him. I still had a powerful case of the maybes. I was feeling greener than ever. And I was just rested enough to be really scared.

But there was no time for agonizing about it. The buses were waiting to take us on our way. There was equipment to draw, equipment to turn in. I threw my gear haphazardly by the handful into my duffel bag. Somewhere along the way I must have been careless, because when I unloaded the stuff later I discovered that I had managed to lose the goddamned knife.

The first stop on the way to the bush was Phuoc Vinh, Cav headquarters, for a week of in-country training. It was a smaller outpost than Long Binh. From where we were quartered you could see the perimeter and beyond it the bush. I began to understand what they meant when they said there was no front and no rear. There were only islands and the sea, and the farther out the tinier the islands.

Strange lessons the lifers taught us at Phuoc Vinh. They were definitely not interested in heroes. John Wayne was a term of derision. They were indoctrinating us in survival, and we were not hard to sell. They taught us how to set up Claymores, how to blow a booby trap. They taught us the art of escape and evasion. E and E, they called it. When all else fails, men, you gonna want to E and E, and that means haul ass outa there. Of course, their interest in our survival was not entirely selfless. It was because of the way the game was scored, body for body.

The worst thing about the lessons was the way

they corrupted you with hope: Three hundred sixty-five days or life, whichever came first. Time was the enemy. Time was the objective. And so we had calendars in our pockets, calendars scratched into our steel-pots, elaborate calendars in our heads. We divided up the year a hundred different ways, triangulating on the seasons, on holidays, on the phases of the moon. The army counted corpses, but we counted days. And if both measures seem to have left out something important, well, maybe that was part of the problem.

After the week's training I was assigned to a battalion headquartered in Quan Loi, which turned out to be little more than a strip of buildings around an airfield, an atoll. I stayed there only a matter of hours.

"Sit on it," the helicopter door gunner shouted as I climbed aboard for the trip into the deep bush.

"Huh?"

"That flak jacket ain't gonna do you no good around your shoulders," he said.

I still didn't understand him, so he got up next to my ear and screamed over the chopper's clatter.

"When you're up in the air," he said, "Charlie ain't gonna be interested in your heart or your mind. He's gonna be firing up at your balls."

I got it straight this time, and I put the jacket where it would do the most good as we soared out over the dark green jungles. We had been in the air for about ten minutes when the door gunner slapped me on the arm and pointed to a thin plume of bright red smoke rising amid the trees. We circled, and I saw a small clearing. A soldier stood near the smoke canister, his fatigues hanging loosely from his shoulders. He held his M-16 above his head with one hand on the barrel and the other on the stock and, like a puppeteer manipulating a marionette, he slowly guided the chopper down.

I jumped out into the high grass and looked around for somebody to report to. The chopper lifted off, and as the sound of its rotors faded into the distance, I heard a voice say, "Well, the chickenshits finally sent us a fresh one." It was my new company commander. He did not detain me long. He looked me up and down and said, "Shake-and-bake, are you? Well, you better be good." Then he sent me off across the clearing to a platoon he said needed all the help it could get.

It did not take me long to learn why. When I found the platoon leader, he was giving a guy an Article 15 for failing to shave. He seemed to want to frighten the man. In time, I discovered that he scared the shit out of everyone, but it wasn't because of nonjudicial punishment.

He insisted on being called Lieutenant Peters, very formal. He was new in country, less than a month. Stocky and nervous, he had all the presence of an insurance salesman. Even if you couldn't see how new he was from the look in his eyes, you could tell by the deep, unfaded color of his fatigues. He wore them properly, bloused at the ankles, sleeves rolled up neatly, pockets all buttoned and accounted for. If he wanted to distinguish his appearance from his men's, he succeeded. But if he wanted to set an example, he was a fool. The grunts were willing to follow an example, even an officer's—but only if it was something that would save their lives, lighten their load, season their C-rations or make their shit run a little thicker than pea soup or a little less constantly than the Mekong River.

The biggest problem the grunts had with Lieutenant Peters was that he was a coward. Not that he didn't take chances. He did, foolish chances. From his height of terror all dangers looked the same. Rebuke from a superior frightened him as much as gunfire. Risk flattened out like a landscape from a climbing jet.

"No sweat," said Davis, the radioman in my squad. "He get out of line, we get him back into it." And then he patted the stock of his rifle.

For the first couple of weeks we humped day after day through the elephant grass and plots of rubber. The land was empty. The sun beat down. I began to smell, then I got used to my smell. Humping my equipment wore me down every day. But every morning I woke up just that much stronger. I got used to the insects, struck bargains with the ground where I slept. I got to know my main men.

Davis was savvy, brown and strong, and they called him Mr. Kool for the cigarettes he favored. His sidekick was a little Spec-4 named Weisman. They were an odd pair. But they had been around for more than seven months, and that meant they were doing something right.

I won't say I felt comfortable out there in the bush, the crud growing in my crotch. And yet nobody was shooting at us, and we weren't shooting at anybody. As far as I was concerned that was the very definition of peace. Then late one afternoon Lieutenant Peters announced that we would be combat-assaulting in the morning, and my personal armistice came to an end.

Neumann and I had gone through the drill often enough in training: Jump from the chopper's skids, run, hit the dirt. I had learned Neumann's way, which was never to hesitate. He saw the place he wanted to reach and dove right in. And in training, I had made a pretty good show of aggressiveness myself. I had howled like a maniac, dodged imaginary incoming until my shadow couldn't keep up with the moves. But the exercises were like practicing swimming strokes on the carpet. Assaulting a hot landing zone, that was a different thing altogether. That was definitely the deep water.

I wished Neumann were there to talk about it that day. I had a hundred questions to ask him about it, and a few of them may even have had answers. I cast about for someone else who might help. Davis and Weisman were preparing fighting holes. Word was out that there were NVA in the area, and the chances were good that they already knew of our plans.

"Just like the dinks to come in and tussle us tonight," said Davis.

"Don't you go waking me up unless it's the fall offensive," said Weisman. "I need my beauty sleep."

They joked about it, but they dug the holes deep that evening. And Davis got on the horn with the artillery base to preplan missions all around us on the probable avenues of approach, just in case. They set out Claymores and cleared fields of fire in the high grass where it pressed in on us. They were ready.

But I did not want to go to them for advice. I was supposed to be their leader. It just wouldn't have been right. So instead I lighted on Perez.

"Combat assault ain't so bad," said the big Mexican squad leader through his thick black moustache. I had been watching him for weeks, fascinated by the way he ran his men. He never seemed to have to say a word.

"Ain't bad at all. . . . You do what you got to do," he said, very slowly, a phrase at a time. "Mr. Kool, he will help you. . . . Good man. . . . It's a lot better than humping."

He spit on the ground, rubbed it in with his foot. Paused.

"Don't be first out," he said. He ran his fingers slowly back and forth on the stock of his rifle. Then he stopped.

"You hwant to see where your squad is going," he said. ". . . Then you can lead them there."

We were camped on the slopes of a wide valley, holding the high ground. Dark had hardly fallen when a firefight erupted miles away on the opposite hills. I was standing first guard, and I watched the red and green tracers crosshatching the blackness, the mortar rounds flashing, the flares flickering down like Christmas stars. When my watch ended and Davis's began, the fight was still going on. I hunkered down in the hole and tried to sleep, but I could still feel the dull thudding of high-explosive rounds resonating through the earth like a pulse. Even after the shelling stopped, I had a hard time relaxing, so I sat up with Davis, doubling our eyes and ears.

Everything was quiet in our sector. The listening posts checked in at regular intervals, clicking their radio handsets twice to signal that all was safe. We saw no movement, heard nothing but the wind in the grass.

Finally, Davis turned the radio over to the men in the next hole and we settled down for the last few hours of the night. I had dreams. Off and on I woke up and only remembered being afraid. But the last dream lingered in those strange moments when you come half-awake in the darkness before dawn and don't know where in the hell you are.

In the dream I was in training back in the World. It was summer, and the air was incredibly close. We started noticing a peculiar smell. At first we thought it was gas from the swamps blowing our way, but then the wind shifted and the stink did not fade. We laughed about it, blamed each other, asked who had farted. But the smell got stronger, and one by one we realized: The smell was death.

We searched all over for the origin, but we couldn't find anything. We washed our clothes, took showers, scrubbed down the walls and floors. But it only got worse. And at night, when the wind died down, it made us gag.

Neumann was the only one who did not seem spooked by it. He went about his business as usual, played his blues at night on the steps, easy as you please. Finally, I asked him what the smell meant, how he could stand it. He was ready to tell me. I was sure that he was. But before I could get him to explain, I woke up.

The sky was dim and gray, and the stench stayed in my nostrils, a memory. I turned my face to the earth and tried to sleep again, but the smell was too strong. I sat up slowly in the hole, raked my face with my hands. That was when I saw it staring at me, no more than a foot away.

It was the skull of a man, and it lay there cradled in an American helmet. The eyes were gone. The bone was almost clean, but there was still enough flesh on it that it stank of decay.

Davis sat upright as I burst out of the hole. The laager came alive. Somebody near me let off a couple of rounds and I fell to the ground. Lieutenant Peters hurried over, stopped the firing, lifted me up.

"Get your shit together, Sergeant," he said.

Davis stepped in between us.

"Maybe you better see what the dinks left us last night," he said, "before you start chewin' anybody's ass."

Peters followed him back to our hole, and when he saw it, he turned so pale that I thought he was going to puke. Then Weisman came up from the perimeter and took a good long look at the skull.

"They turned the Claymores around on us," he said. "If anybody had heard them coming in and blown a mine, it would have exploded right back into his face."

"Man," said Davis. "I thought I'd seen everything."

"They were close enough to cut my throat," I said.

"There must not have been more than a couple of them," Weisman said. "Otherwise, they would have raised some hell for sure."

He said it as if he thought it should give me some kind of comfort. But it didn't. I just stood there looking at the severed head, unable to take my eyes off it, the bone bleeding in the red light of dawn, the eye sockets as wide as terror, the helmet resting at an obscene, jaunty angle across the brow. If Neumann were here, I told myself, he would say it only proved how careful we had to be, how good they were at infiltration. He would say that it was a lesson, and that this time it had come cheap. He would have tamed the thing somehow. I knew he would have.

"Looks too big to belong to a Vietnamese," said Weisman. "I guess we ought to police it up and send it to the rear. They might be able to identify it, give it a proper burial."

But I was not about to order anybody to do it, let alone touch the thing myself. In the end, Weisman took care of it. He wrapped the skull up in a poncho and called in a Medevac. The chopper came from the other side of the valley carrying a load of fresh bodies in bags. It barely touched down to pick up our offering, and then it was gone.

"It may have been somebody's buddy," Weisman said, as if he had to excuse what he had done. "It may have been somebody's son."

When it came time to move out, the squad formed up around me and we went to the LZ. Somebody in the first platoon popped smoke—billowing red—

and I heard the low stammering of the choppers before they reared up over the treeline. We were to assault a platoon at a time, and ours was to be second in. The first platoon ducked under the pounding rotors and climbed aboard. The men moved like robots. Anything more animate would have balked. Then the big machines lifted and roared up over our heads.

When the choppers returned for us, Peters's radio man popped the smoke. And as we climbed in, Davis pointed to something on the bird's side. But Weisman was gently pushing me from behind, and so I did not get a look at what Davis was trying to show me. His black face was beaded with sweat as he climbed in next to me. He said something urgently, but I couldn't understand it for the noise. I leaned toward him. Our steel-pots cracked together.

"See them bullet holes in the door?" he said. "They're fresh. Fuckin' LZ is hot."

The chopper shook and strained and hovered a few feet off the ground. Then it moved forward with a jerk, and I lurched into Weisman. He took me by the arm, and I will be forever grateful for that touch.

The choppers flew slowly in formation, tail to nose, bobbing in sequence. Below us the land seemed utterly empty. I couldn't imagine anything living in that darkness. But then a billow of smoke jumped up from the jungles. Then another. I thought I heard the rush of a shell come past us.

Off in the distance two sleek Cobra gunships turned wide circles on the spot where the shells were landing. Then one of them angled toward the earth, slowly tipping and turning until its nose pointed downward like a dive bomber. At that precise moment its sides erupted in smoke. It seemed to stop dead in the sky. Its rockets pierced the green with a noiseless burst of fire. Then it soared back upward as its mate began its own chassé of death.

We continued to lose altitude, and the door gunners leaned far out over their weapons. Weisman shifted his bandoleers of M-60 machine-gun bullets, fingered them lightly, fastidiously. Davis grabbed for the antenna of his radio. I checked the clip of my rifle, flicked it onto rock and roll.

As we neared the ground, the gunners opened up on the treeline. The pilot hovered five or six feet from the ground. He held there steadily as Weisman and Davis edged onto the skids in front of me. They balanced for a moment, then leaped. I slid to the door and followed.

I jumped. Fell to my knees. Staggered up. Ran toward the first little rise I could find. I grabbed at the grass and pulled tightly against the berm. The choppers lifted off, and their guns became quieter as they moved away. But there was other gunfire that did not fade. Somebody was shooting back.

I had no idea where the fire was coming from. It lashed our position, and nobody was about to raise his head to satisfy my curiosity. Davis was working the radio. Weisman lay on his side facing me, his thumb ticking the safety of his rifle back and forth as steadily as the movements of a clock. Off to our right, the fire seemed heavier. That was where the first platoon had gone in.

Cobras wheeled over our position and fired into

the treeline. I watched the fire bloom over the tops of the trees, and it was even more beautiful than when I had watched it from above. This time it was a fiery garland of life.

I had lost all sense of time and direction. I knew I was supposed to be leading, but I did not dare to move. Then, as if by some superior command, every man in the field shifted ground. Without a word being spoken, the whole unit slid forward like a reptile on a rock. It was just something that happened. Spread over fifty meters of obscuring terrain, somehow we were one.

We continued to move ahead. It may have been toward the danger, for all I knew. But this was not heroism. We did not get to our feet and charge. Dumb, insensate organism that we were, we just inched forward toward the treeline ahead where the artillery was crashing in.

When we reached a gully, we stopped and spaced out evenly along it. There was a kind of territorial imperative working: Nobody wanted to be close enough to another man to invite a mortar round. Some of the men braced their weapons on the lip of the bank and fired off short bursts into the dark wall of jungle ahead of us. The shots sounded tiny in the wide field, popping firecrackers. Then the artillery came thundering in again, and wingers sang in the air above us.

Once more the moment came and we began to advance like a great serpent—now the head, now the belly, now the tail—until we reached a patch of high grass. Weisman disappeared into it and then materialized again a few meters ahead of me.

Davis's voice was there, but for a time I lost his body. They came and went like apparitions.

Our rifles were useless here. We moved by momentum, not by will, for in the dense vegetation there was no forward, no back. When we finally broke out of the grass, the firing was all ours. I could see another unit spread out, pouring fire from the right. Davis slid in next to me. "First platoon took some hits," he said. "Three wounded. One dead. There's the Medevac."

I watched the chopper wheel in on a plume of bright green smoke. Two men carried one of the wounded to it, crouching as they ran. Two other wounded men hobbled after them under their own power. Finally, the fourth: They carried him roughly, slung between them like a sack.

"They think there may be snipers," Davis said. "We better stay put." But then Peters got on the horn and ordered us to move into the treeline, and to my astonishment, we went.

"Wants to search for bodies," said Davis, staying close to me now.

"There it is," said Weisman.

But we did not find any corpses that day. Lieutenant Peters reported some blood trails, and Davis said under his breath that that was a lot of shit. The first platoon came up with a dozen dead in their sector of the bush, and the colonel passed the word from his command chopper overhead that he was pleased. A textbook encounter, he called it. Best fighting machine in the war, he said. Bunch of fuckin' animals.

When we finished the search, we took a position on the edge of the jungle and threw down our equipment. I lighted up a cigarette and offered Perez some of my Kool-Aid. He said he'd stick with plain water.

"Like I tol' you," he said, drawing his canteen out of its canvas pouch. "You got to do it . . . and you do."

"I didn't even fire a round," I said.

"Don't worry," he said, and took a pull of water. "It comes natural." He tipped the canteen in my direction, gesturing toward my rifle with it. "Natural as a baby sucking tit."

In the field they delivered the mail whenever we needed to be resupplied with something else. And when they did, I always got my share. My parents went on about this and that, who was getting married, who had moved into the neighborhood, how I should try to be careful. My friend Richard Herring kept me up to date on what he knew about Sharon, which was mercifully little. He also let me in on each of his new phases. Richard's ideas were like illnesses. When he had one, he could not think of anything else. But when he got over it, he could hardly remember what it was that had troubled him so. At first he was into behaviorism. Then the metaphysical poets. Lately he had been lecturing me at length about the I Ching.

I kept up my side of the correspondence, but it was hard to make connections between their world and mine. So I simply told reassuring lies. It isn't so bad, really. I've made some good friends. That sort of thing. Some guys tried to send home ears lopped off the NVA dead. Maybe that was more to the point.

I had also sent several letters to Neumann, but for a long time I had not heard from him. We were on standdown in Quan Loi when I finally got an envelope with the 82nd Airborne's markings on it. I opened it eagerly. Neumann's letter was spare. It simply said that his unit was going home but he was not. They were sending him to the Cav.

"All right," I said aloud.

"What's that?" said Davis.

"The guy I told you about is coming to the Cav."

"Cav's a big place," said Davis. "Cav's a continent."

Neumann and a guy named Jackpot were going to sign up for special duty, the letter said. Jackpot's brother-in-law had done it a year before and talked it up.

"He's volunteering for a Blue Team," I said.

"Crazy motherfucker," said Davis.

"Fed up with cherry lieutenants is why," I said.

"He sure got that right," said Weisman.

"Wants me to volunteer, too. He wants me to join him."

There would be advantages, of course. I would be with Neumann again. I might feel a measure of control. At least I'd get away from this big, stumbling rifle company humping along like a beast of burden waiting to be whipped.

Davis pulled out some Chiclets, popped them

into his mouth, then looked at Weisman, who was weaving himself a lucky bracelet out of twine.

"You gonna do it?" said Davis. "You gonna split on us?"

Weisman looked up from his braiding and shook his head.

"What do you mean asking a thing like that? He has brothers here, Mr. Kool. You don't walk out on family."

That was one reason I decided against taking Neumann up on it. But there were others. I won't say that I enjoyed my job, but I knew what to expect. The big dumb beast might be slow-witted, but at least I could keep up with it. Blue Teams were different animals altogether. When a chopper fell in hostile territory, the Blues went in to secure it. When somebody spotted a cluster of NVA soldiers in the open, they flew the Blues out to occupy them. If somebody smelled an ambush brewing, the Blues dropped in to spring it. The Blues did not go humping in the bush. Their trips were quick, but when they went somewhere, it was worth going.

I folded Neumann's letter in two, then in four, then in eight. I tucked it into the plastic case where I kept my cigarettes and cash. The Blues were Neumann's way, not mine. I took what was given. I only did what I had to do.

Two days later the standdown in Quan Loi came to an end. The choppers took us into an empty plain up along the Cambodian border west of the camp. Off in the distance an endless forest rose on the horizon. We humped all day and reached the edge of it late in the afternoon.

It was a bad march. The sun beat down from directly overhead. No clouds eased it, and there was no shade. It only took a few hours before the soothing effects of the standdown were gone. I was soaked with sweat and could feel the rot growing again on my balls. I chewed salt to stave off exhaustion. My throat clogged with dust. My legs went weak under my load.

When we finally reached the treeline, Lieutenant Peters gave us a break. I stopped where I stood, threw off my equipment and fell flat on the ground. But I only had time to get the numbness out of my legs when Peters ordered us to saddle up and move into the jungle. We worked our way slowly through the vines and tangles of underbrush. The darkness under the three-tiered vegetation was scattered with shards of light that somehow found their way through. Branches and sharp leaves ripped at my face and the backs of my hands. The air under the thick blanket of leaves was viscous, sour with decay. I stumbled on a hidden vine. I cursed. It was worse than the long hump in the clearing. Here you couldn't even develop a rhythm, a momentum to carry you through. Every moment you had to fight the better judgment of your limbs.

Dusk was coming. The bright patches of sunlight dimmed. The jungles grew more vague. Still the heat did not subside. I was pissed off that we had moved into the trees so late, so tired. Maybe it was Peters's fault. Or maybe it was just part of the great mechanical design of the Green Machine. Maybe there was just no stopping it once it got started. Or maybe if you looked at it from far enough away it all made some sense. But none of that mattered to me. All that mattered was the sweat, the muscles aching and the retreating promise of rest.

After a while my squad moved up into the lead, and I took the point myself. I had to cut the trail. My hands grew raw from the machete and the rough bark of the vine. We weren't going anywhere as far as I could tell. We were just going.

Davis stayed close behind me, incautiously close. But the jungle was so thick and it haunted me so much that I was glad to have him there. I crouched to get under a thick vine. Davis tapped my shoulder. I froze. He pointed to our right. I expected a tripwire, but he was only pointing to an overgrown trail just barely visible through the tangle. I shook my head no. He nodded, and we moved off away from it.

A few minutes later Peters called a halt. I drank a touch of warm, rubbery canteen water and downed some more salt. The cloth band around my head was soaked, and my eyes stung with sweat. The jungles muttered softly. I heard footfalls coming up behind us, but I did not see Peters until he loomed over me. He took off his steel-pot and knelt down beside us.

"Cut over to the right," he whispered. "An old trail. We'll make some time, get the hell out of this shit before dark."

A few tiny gnats played along the matted hair on his forehead. He refused to meet my eyes.

"We'll be moving out in five," he said, and

started to stand. Davis stood up first, and I saw his hand clenched on the stock of his rifle.

"We're not taking the trail," I said. "It's ambush country."

"What's that, Sergeant?" Peters said.

"We're going out the back way."

Davis stood above Peters. I shifted my weight and looked at the ground. All the logic of survival and all the power were on my side. Davis stepped back a pace. I heard the click of his safety going off. Peters heard it, too. He shot a look at Davis and then came back to me. Logic and power were not enough.

"You'll do what I order, Sergeant," he said.

We could have taken him right there, either one of us, and he knew it.

"The trail's grown over," he said. "I know what I'm doing. The colonel wants us to make time."

Davis questioned me with his eyes. I answered by looking away. Peters moved back to the rest of the platoon.

Minutes later we broke onto the path. Goddamnit, I gave in because I was not sure. For myself alone it would have been one thing. But for all those others, for the platoon, for the company, for whatever other men were counting on us, I could not have known. All I knew was that when we moved we moved and when we stopped we stopped. That whatever propelled us was beyond our control, and you were a fool to challenge it.

I was still green. Very green. We moved up the trail.

Then everything exploded behind me. I fell and turned to my belly in one motion. Davis staggered in the smoke fifteen meters back. He dropped to his side. The antenna of his radio slapped the trees. The jungle burned with AK and machine-gun fire.

They had let me through. The bastards had let me through and sprung the ambush behind me.

That was when my bowels let go. I remember moving toward the firing. I remember throwing grenades. I remember the shooting going on forever. Then I was lying across the roots of a high tree and firing clip after clip into the shadows.

When the silence came, I got back to the trail where Davis lay. He was on the ground, shrouded in smoke, his legs tangled up under him. I moved closer.

"Mr. Kool," said Perez, leaning over him. "Mr. Fucking Kool." He lifted Davis's steel-pot. One side was shattered. Half of Davis's head had ripped through it.

A few meters farther back another man was down on the trail. I moved toward him and saw that it was Weisman. The front of his shirt was black with blood. I lifted his hand. It was limp.

"Forget about him," said the medic. "He's gone."

I stood up and walked past where Peters was crouched over his map, talking into the radio. I walked straight past without a word.

The dinks had been just waiting for us to take the trail. They had sprung an L ambush on us. I should have tripped a booby trap as I came up behind them. But I did not. They fucked up, that's all. So did we. And somebody paid. The dinks, Davis, Weisman. Simple statement of fact. They were dead and I was not. But that fact did something to you. It made you feel terrible for what you did not feel.

Peters kept jabbering away on the radio, and the rest of the platoon was moving around aimlessly. There was an open space in the vines to the right. I made my way into it.

It led to a hollow in the jungle that ran parallel to the trail, arched over by the high trees. The light beamed down in great motes swirling with smoke. I stripped down my pants and kneeled to clean them with leaves. When I finished, I walked deeper into the bower. Then I stopped short.

A few steps away from me at the farthest end of the hollow lay three men, partially hidden by the camouflage they had set up around their machine gun. They wore tan NVA uniforms, the men I killed. Flies gathered in their blood, and across one of the dead men's eyes, open in the final terror, marched a scouting party of ants.

All at once it seemed to me that the Green Machine was a lie. And you could not blame nature for what we had done. Nature was the decay and bloat of the corpses and the ants moving to rid the jungles of the stink of our work.

Nothing kept me in this platoon anymore. My brothers were dead. I had let myself be carried along by my idea of necessity, and they had died. I had seen the way death wove its way in when you did not struggle against the binding. And now it was time to try Neumann's way.

# 3
# The Blues

My last weeks in Lieutenant Peters's platoon were painful. I resented the replacements they sent for Weisman and Davis. I rode them so hard that Peters complimented me. The bastard. I could not stand to look at the man.

When they finally cut my orders and brought me in from the bush, I tried at once to find Neumann. But somebody said he was off with a detail pulling security, so I reported to the Blue Team's platoon leader, Lieutenant Thomas Selder. He was much older than any of the rest of us. At first I did not know what to think of that. An old lieutenant could either be a dud who missed his promotions or an ex-grunt up from the ranks. Selder certainly looked enough like a grunt, weatherbeaten as a stump. When I entered the hootch, he was cleaning his nails with a familiar-looking hunting knife. After I introduced myself, he gave me a broad grin, took the knife by its point and flung it past me. I turned. It vibrated in a beam like a tuning fork.

"Wasn't trying to do a number on you," he said, seeing that I was giving the knife a pretty good eye. "That's just where I keep it stowed. Pretty fancy item, eh? Definitely not government issue."

"Roger that, sir."

"You a lifer, Morgan?"

"Pardon me, sir?"

"A lifer," he said. "Take it easy. I'm not going to ask you to reenlist. I just want to know where you're coming from."

I told him the unit name.

"Literal bastard," he said. "Got to be a draftee. College grad, right?"

"Yes, sir."

"I'm a lifer, Morgan," he said. "But as far as I'm concerned, draftee or Regular Army, it don't make a matter about a man. They drafted me, too, the first time."

"When was that, sir?"

"When you thought war was a kid's game, son," he said. "They drafted me back when all they had in this hole were a bunch of sorry-ass advisers. Sorry wasn't the word for it. But there I was, a swinging dick like you, ready for glory."

"I'm not expecting much glory, sir," I said.

"Smarter than I was. I guess nobody's got any cherry to lose anymore."

He sat down on the edge of his bunk and nodded me down onto a footlocker across from him.

"The worst you heard back in the World about how it was then? It wasn't the half of it. We didn't even have decent maps. They were all in French.

Couldn't read them. The newspapers said we didn't know where we were going in Vietnam. Hell, we didn't even know where the fuck we were standing."

Lieutenant Selder stood up and scratched his arm under where the sleeve was rolled up. High on his bicep there was a greenish patch that might once have been a heart and a woman's name. Next to it a long scar gashed toward the elbow.

"I'll tell you one thing," he said, leaning toward me, his face drawn, afire. "It's different in the Blues. It's clean. It's righteous."

He coughed, ran his hand through his graying brush cut and then reached under his bunk and pulled out a battered old briefcase.

"I been with this unit six months now," he said, pulling out a piece of paper. "Got written down here the name of every KIA we've had. I take it out from time to time to remind me how they died. They fucked up, that's what happened. They fucked up or somebody else did. That's how people get greased . . . except maybe Sanchez. That was different. But you get the point."

"Yes, sir."

"Well, nobody dies anymore. We got it together in this platoon. The other men, they'll keep you alive because they know you'll do the same for them. You can count on them. Every one. Simple as that. Come on, I'll take you to meet them."

They were hanging around a hootch down the way, a bunch of bandits.

"Look at them," said the LT. "They kind of favor them bandanas. Here's something to remember. In this unit, we don't sweat the small stuff.

But don't you ever let us down when it counts. Don't ever. That's the bargain."

"Yes, sir," I said as we reached them.

"A new stud for our farm," the LT said.

"Some stud farm," one of the men drawled. "When you gonna put us out for breeding?"

"Way I hear it, you're working on that aspect of the military experience all by your own self, Jackpot," said the LT.

Then he started to introduce me around. There was tiny Diaz and Tender, the radioman who asked me to call him by the name on his birth certificate, which was Ambrose. I told him I would, but I never did. There was Bones the medic, Angelo and Reed.

Out from behind a hootch walked a skinny grunt with pale skin burnt crimson and pebbled like a farmer's neck. It was Thompson, and he looked at me as if I could not have been dumber.

"This here's Canary," said Jackpot, introducing an Oriental grunt. "He's Japanese, but he ain't no gook."

"Not this war," said Thompson. "How you doin', Morgan? I been wonderin' how long it would take before you came tailin' after Neumann."

"You know each other?" said the LT.

"Small world," I said.

Jackpot offered to help me process into the unit, and we headed off toward the headquarters hootches. He ambled down the road in no particular hurry, every now and then spitting into the dust and then stopping to kick dirt over it as a dog would. He had a long, Ho Chi Minh moustache, and in place of the regulation olive-drab jungle bonnet, he wore a madras golf hat bleached out by the sun. Under it, he had the face of a boy. But the eyes, they belonged to somebody else's movie: black and white, maybe even silent, that old.

He didn't talk about what it was he had seen to give him such eyes, and I didn't ask, because on the surface he was one of those guys who seem to take things much easier than they are. He greased my way past the supply sergeant, who issued me camouflage fatigues Jackpot called Can't See Me Suits. He sped me through the medic's check. And when the finance clerk told me my records were so screwed up it would take days to straighten them out and get me my pay, Jackpot just pointed to the gecko on the wall and drawled, "Did you know that if you grab one of those Fuck You lizards by the tail, he just lets go and walks away? Guess that's how they got their name. I'll be damned if anything is impossible."

"Crazy grunts," said the clerk.

"Anything that gets you through the day," said Jackpot.

The clerk just smiled, shook his head and straightened me out in record time.

By the time I got cleaned up and into my new fatigues, it was getting dark. I heard the sad jazz before I actually saw him. It was coming from out back behind the hootches, and I followed it. Neumann was sitting against one of the bunkers, hunched over his flute. Jackpot and Diaz were there, too. So was a brother I had not met.

Neumann couldn't see me at first. I watched from the shadows. He leaned against the bleached green sandbags as the sun died behind him. The notes were slow and mournful, lonely. It was odd how melancholy his music could be. Neumann did not reveal that side any other way.

I stepped out of the shadows and he finally noticed me.

"Don't stop now," said the brother. "You cookin'. Ain't no rests in this music here. Ain't no rest at all."

Neumann grabbed my hand. A bright cross-hatched scar the color of a bruise angled across the back of his wrist. I turned his hand to look at it.

"Got my Purple Heart already," he said. "It was easy."

"When?" I asked.

"Couldn't have been too long ago, could it?" he said. "No more than a lifetime."

"There it is," the brother chanted.

"You all met my man Morgan?" Neumann said.

"I ain't," said the brother, sticking out his hand. "I'm from Cleveland, the bad part."

"What do they call you?" I asked.

"Mister," he said, dark and basso.

"Shee-it, Jones," said Jackpot. "What's this man gonna think?"

"You got another stick?" said Jones. "That'll help clear his mind."

Jackpot pulled out a package of local cigarettes—Park Lanes—and lighted one up. I sat down on the sandbags and Jackpot passed it to me. It wasn't Kentucky burley.

"They make them this way?" I asked. "Filters and all?"

"Little women in back rooms empty the tobacco out," said Jackpot. "Put the good stuff in. You don't see these tailor-mades much in the bush. Only in Saigon. But we got us a connection. There's *nothing* you can't buy in Saigon."

I must have started to look nervous as the smoke wafted toward the hootches, because Neumann broke in and said, "Nobody hassles us. The LT only has one rule: Be straight at first light. That's when we do our work. The other lifers, they just stay away."

"We so *bad*," said Jones. "This here dude even come off playing his flute, and I ain't heard nobody calling him a pussy."

"Except maybe Thompson," said Diaz.

"He got no ear," said Jones.

"None but the ones he takes off dinks," said Jackpot.

The grass made them all laugh at that, and damned if I didn't laugh, too. A little uncomfortable about it, maybe, fighting it back. But I laughed. I laughed.

"That was some good music you were playing before," I finally said. "Very sad sounds."

"You should have been here a week ago," said Neumann, moving back, hiding. "We had a guy with an acoustic guitar. Wild chords. But he isn't here anymore."

"Dead?" I asked.

The others traded looks. You tried to spare yourself the word at least, when the thing itself was always so close. I was sorry that I said it, but there it was, squatting among us, leering.

"He just shipped home," said Neumann. "Didn't the LT tell you? Nobody has to die."

"Everybody do," said Jones.

Something flickered across Neumann's face. I'd never seen it so clearly there before, the pain. Then he took a big hit off the joint and passed it on. Jackpot lighted another to get two going around simultaneously.

"Got it, flaunt it," Diaz said.

"You should have seen him in Saigon," Jackpot said. "For me, it was short-time city, steam and cream. Fifteen minutes, squirt and good-bye. But Neumann here had something regular. Jesus, she was sweet. Classy, too. Educated. Even had tits. She was a dink, but she had tits like any white woman."

"That pale and sickly?" said Jones. "No wonder she had to settle for a grunt."

"If you had it so good, why you come up here to the bad bush?" said Diaz.

"Something happened," Jackpot said. "Ask Neumann."

We all turned to him for an answer, then seeing ourselves move in unison, mechanical soldiers, we all began to laugh because it seemed such a silly cartoon stoned.

"You gonna tell us?" Jones finally asked for the rest of us.

"I wanted into a good unit," said Neumann. "Had a bad day."

"Bad enough to get him the Silver Star," said Jackpot.

"Outasight," said Diaz, "a regular war hero."

"Bronze, silver, gold," rumbled Jones. "Some fuckin' Olympics."

"Vietnam marathon," said Diaz. "You finish, you win."

We all giggled stupidly, but not out of disrespect for the medal. We knew they did not give the silver one to a grunt unless he had really done something. But what else could you do except laugh?

After the snickering died down, we lapsed into a spaced-out silence. The heat and humidity closed in. Our smiles corroded. Our hearts sank down. The bats quarreled in the trees.

It was Diaz who finally asked it again.

"How'd you get the star?"

"He don't like to talk about it," said Jackpot.

"Tell you what," said Neumann, "let's all just sit around and tell each other war stories. You know, how we almost bought the farm and how other guys did, with the big down payment."

It was bitter, but everyone respected it. Neumann stood and headed toward the hootches.

"Hey, brother," said Jones. "Ain't you gonna play no more jazz?"

"It'd just be noise," he said, almost whispering, and then he walked away.

At first nobody said anything. Then Jones said, "Shit." And that was apology enough for all of us.

Jackpot was fumbling with some soggy matches.

"What happened?" I asked him. "How did he get that medal?"

"The dinks got into a little ville one night," he said. "You got any dry matches? These here are like trying to light a banana."

He could not stop laughing. I gave him the matches and waited for him to calm down.

"So Charlie got into a ville," I said.

"Blew it away," he said.

"You were there?"

"Next morning we were. We moved in at first light. Nothing left but smoldering junk. The only somebodies alive were an old man and a little boy.

"Neumann picked the kid up and rode him around on his shoulders. Nobody knew what else to do with him. All his people were dead.

"Pretty soon here comes a psy-ops major, pleased as can be because he's got him a real big massacre and this time it was the other side did it for a change. With him are two or three photographers. They had hardly started snapping, though, when the dinks attacked again."

"In daylight?" asked Diaz.

"Bet your ass in daylight," he said. "They must have had a main-force company. They had blown away the ville to set a trap for us. They knew we'd roll in to see if we could help. They knew we'd look around and see what we could do. They knew we'd get all wrought up and start carrying ten-year-old kids around on our shoulders like Dutch uncles. You got to understand, the dinks know exactly who we are.

"First came the mortars. The CO, the forward observer, the platoon leader, the whole bunch of them bought it in the first couple minutes. The rest of us just got down low and waited for somebody to kill us or either to tell us how to stay alive."

"That would be Neumann," I said.

"Roger that," he said. "He found the RTO, got on the horn and started calling in artillery and air. By then the dinks were moving in right on top of us. They came up behind the mortars. Neumann sent the whole company E and Eing out of there, but he stayed forward with the RTO to see how the thing would develop. Finally, he walked the artillery up real close, brought in napalm—took some burns himself it was so close. Then he called in the last mission on his own position and tore ass out of there. The RTO got greased, but Neumann made it somehow with just some shrapnel in the hand. We were fifty percent casualties that day."

"What happened to the little boy?" asked Diaz.

"Who the hell knows?"

My mouth was dry. It wasn't only the grass. Hell, the grass didn't have anything to do with it.

Jackpot held a smoking joint out in front of him and sniffed at it.

"Something must be wrong with this pack," he said. "I don't feel this shit at all anymore."

It wasn't exactly like still being stoned when I woke up the next morning in the dark. The high was gone, and only the chemical fear was left. Jackpot was snoring. Neumann was still deep in sleep. Time had returned to the old slow moan. The shadows on the walls were not beautiful. And nothing seemed very funny at all.

Even before the LT came, I knew something was wrong. I was mistaken; I thought it was paranoia. Then I heard his voice.

"Let's crank," he said. "We got contact."

"Sweet Jesus," I said. "So soon?"

Outside, as we moved toward the chopper pad, Thompson pointed enthusiastically to the red, setting moon, a raw wound in the sky above the trees.

"Deep shit today for sure," he said.

The Blues mumbled agreement, and I could not dispute it. Blood on the moon meant somebody would die in the bush. Them or us, just somebody. It might seem silly to you, but these things were true. Just as seeing monkeys meant life. But you didn't see many monkeys anymore. Like the birds, most had died under the bombs. Fog, naturally, was a bad sign, very bad. Their eyes could penetrate it. Ours could not. This was something given, genetic, a racial weakness we all acknowledged.

We laid fear's usual burden on talismans. Neumann had his bright silver flute; he shined it every day. Jackpot wore a small cloth bag on a thong around his neck. He said it contained hair from his special girl's most special place. Thompson collected names. He claimed his kills and searched the dead for identification. He kept a list of his victims and had it with him each time he went into the bush. "My own personal army," he said. And then there was Diaz. He had a common gold cross on a chain. But that was all right, too. We grunts were ecumenical as hell.

As we waited on the chopper pad, the base camp was still, the insect hum broken only by occasional meaningless machine-gun bursts on the perimeter. Mad minutes, they called it. The random firing was supposed to scare away sappers. All it did that I could tell was to keep the jungle mowed. The bush kept trying to squeeze in on us, you see, to push us out.

Tender was talking incessantly on the radio. He was by nature a man of few words. But as soon as a mission began, he had the phone to his ear constantly, jabbering away. "Dog Day. This is Lighter Two. Need confirmation at Tango Echo Niner." Calling in coordinates, clearing through to the Medevac net, talking in a radio language with words that stood for letters and letters that were just labels, using letters and numbers that said it all.

The choppers began to whine as the big rotors started slowly to cut through the heavy air. Neumann came at a run from the tactical operations center. "They suspect an ambush," he said, catching his breath.

"Then why go?" I said. I knew we were the Blues and we were bad, but ambushes were wasp nests; you just left them alone.

"Squadron of armor on a road up north," he said. "Bridge out a few klicks ahead of them. Blown last night. They figure the dinks are set up on the near side. Want us to spring the ambush before the tanks move up. No sweat. Close to a place called Xuan The. Ever heard of it?"

"Never have," I said, shouting over the clatter of the choppers testing their lift.

Neumann moved among the men, passing the news. Then we all piled into the choppers, squad by squad. Thompson had brought a cup of coffee with him. As the chopper got light on its skids and floated off, he sat Indian-style on the steel floor, his strong shoulders hunched over as he gazed at the ground. His right cheek twitched wildly, but his face showed no expression at all. A laurel of steam from the cup wreathed his neck.

Tender sat next to me. Out of radio contact while we were in the air, he leaned back, radio clanging against the firewall. He closed his eyes as if he were resting, but I could see them darting back and forth behind the lids.

Angelo and Reed fingered their rifles. Little Diaz with his spindly moustache and rubble of beard sat dead still. After a few minutes with his head bent forward and his hands barely crossed on the clip of his M-16, Diaz lifted his right hand slowly to his forehead, dropped it to his waist, waited, then touched each armpit lightly as if scratching an itch. He wanted to keep his sign of the cross private, to hide it in common gestures.

The chopper fell quickly in spirals. Two Cobras hung low in the air a fair distance away. We wanted surprise. There would be no artillery preparation.

The LZ was a road junction cut into the trees. A stream angled across the bigger of the two roads about fifty meters from the intersection. The ruins of a concrete and steel bridge hung into the stagnant water. The woods had been cut back away from the road, but the jungles were well on their way toward reclaiming the territory.

The choppers landed in two waves. My squad was in the first. I found a raised clump of earth about twenty meters from the choppers and hid behind it. I heard no shooting, only the racket from the helicopters. The second wave of choppers slid in, and a single, evil RPD machine gun opened up from my left across the stream. One chopper faltered as it disgorged its troops. It lurched upward trying to escape, then bucked and fell. I felt the heat of the flames. The whole platoon was returning fire at the sputtering enemy machine gun. Its muzzle flash blinked from a spot across the stream. The LT had it figured right, an ambush set just where the armor would have bunched up to make the ford.

The second chopper got off and the Cobra lashed in for the kill. I moved on my belly toward the smoldering wreck. Tender followed. The machine gun let up, and we made a quick, low dash across the dirt intersection. Neumann was there with the pilot, tying off his arm where he had caught a round. Bones, the medic, crouched over one of the door gunners who was badly burned. Tender called for a Dustoff.

Another machine gun opened up on our left flank, sending us all sprawling for cover. Neumann motioned for my fire as the first of the artillery came in. He threw off his gear and took a grenade launcher from one of the other men. I fired toward the place where we heard the machine gun while Neumann crawled quickly to the bank of the stream. Several other automatic weapons erupted at him. He reached the stump of a tree, aimed the blooker and thumped four grenades into the jungle. On the third, the machine gun stopped firing.

The LT was on the radio telling us to set up a line near the stream. Thompson was next to me, emptying clip after clip into the opposite treeline. I heard the roar of armor somewhere down the road. The Dustoff came and left.

Then the armor column poked into view around a bend a few hundred meters down the road. Two Sheridans and an armored personnel carrier eased around the corner and fired their big guns into the forests on either side of the road. The Cobras circled in a wider arc.

117

"Got a company flanking now—blocking force," Tender yelled.

"Got us some dinks," Thompson cried, and then let go another clip into the trees to help out the tanks' big pieces.

Then the shooting stopped. The armor sat idling. I looked around for Neumann. He was off to my left, and I went to him in a low crouch. He kneeled beside a tree, staring deep into the jungles across the stream. There was a little bit of blood dripping off his chin. It came from a gash under his right eye.

"You're hit," I said. Neumann kept watching the treeline.

"Shaving cut," he said.

"Maybe you'd better . . ."

His open palm caught me on the neck and sent me to the ground. Then he started firing. An explosion ripped through the forests across the stream.

"The stupid sonofabitch," Neumann whispered. "The stupid goddamn sonofabitch."

I got up to my knees. Neumann slouched against the tree. His rifle fell from his hands.

"I saw him move," he said. "The stupid sonofabitch was moving where I could see him."

Tender came up beside us.

"LT says to cross the stream," he said.

Neumann's strength came back to him. He changed clips and we started charily down the steep bank. The creek was narrow and noxious, ankle-deep in slime on the bottom. The water reached my armpits at the deepest spot. When I got to the other side, I saw what Neumann had done.

The tan-clad body of a small NVA soldier lay caught in the crotch of a vine with his baby face hanging open at the jaw. A grenade he had prepared for us had blown him away at the thighs. Flies swarmed in the blood.

Neumann stood over the dead dink's body and did not move. Thompson made his way toward us.

"He got any papers?" Thompson asked, hurrying toward the corpse. Neumann stopped him. Thompson never touched the body. Neumann stood guard over it all morning. He only left when they came to lift us out, and even then only reluctantly.


The first couple of months with the Blues made me think I had made the right decision. We were busy. There was always some mission for us. But we were also very good. The LT didn't have to go around reading every man his part. We improvised, and we got the job done. Self-reliance, that was our strength. And when you got into a tight spot, you could always count on somebody being there to back you up. The dinks seemed to understand. They did not mix with us. They knew how mean we were, we thought. We were the Blues, and we had their minds.

We took some casualties during this lull, but none of them too bad. Neumann always walked point and found the mines and traps. Jones said his damned fillings must have been radar. Tender got nicked by a sniper. They dusted off Reed to the hospital ship, but he was back before my R and R. Thompson's list got a little longer as we raided suspected enemy hiding places and weapons caches.

But then one day the lull came to an end. The accounts were finally called into balance. We were sent to the Circle of Sorrow.

It was a wooded area up near the border. The French had given it its name, and no grunt who had ever been there had come up with a better one. The dinks were dug in. They had bunkers with gunports, not just the usual little spider holes. And for once, when the Blues marched in, the dinks did not scurry. This was our fantasy—getting them to stand and fight—and it turned into a nightmare. They fought, all right. They fought like hell.

The first unit engaged had been a Cav company. The grunts had been humping for a week and had no idea what they were stumbling into. By the time we got there to reinforce them, we could hardly find enough men left to fill a platoon. The dinks had machine guns set up with overlapping fields of fire. They just swept back and forth through the woods like scythes. All a man could do was make love to the loam and hope for the best.

When the guns paused we heard worse, the moaning of the wounded we could not reach. Limb wounds pleading for rescue. Gut wounds pleading for death. The dinks would wait until someone tried to move up and help them. Then they would open up again.

Neumann tried to hold Bones back. He moved from man to man telling us to keep our positions. The LT was calling in artillery. It thundered, shaking the earth under our bellies. It did not dig out the bunkers, but it made the dinks keep their heads down long enough for Neumann and Jones and Jackpot and Bones to drag a few of the worst cases back to where Bones could give them the holy water, morphine.

Eight hours we hung in there, sneaking out the dying, leaving the dead alone. Finally, the relief arrived, U.S. and ARVN together. This was the latest masterplan, we were told. And such things, we were supposed to understand, took time to organize.

As we pulled out, we mourned the Canary. We did not put his body on a Medevac. We kept him with us, rode with him on the chopper, an honor guard. "That was bad luck," the LT said. "He definitely did not fuck up. Not the Canary. It happens."

Harrison had taken two rounds in the arm, an expensive ticket back to the World. Thompson had nothing to show for the battle but a bad case of the shakes. Diaz went to see the chaplain, and Jackpot put another peace symbol on his web gear.

The peace symbols Jackpot and I wore were, of course, different from the ones they put on their book bags and placards back in the World. Our symbol stood for something concrete, immediate. Theirs was an abstraction, and we had pretty much given up on flags. We did not care about history or intentions. We did not even worry who was right and who was wrong. We were not looking for a lull or de-escalation or anything else that might not last. The only bombing that bothered us was a mission whose rounds fell short. And the only problem with free-fire zones was that the other side was free to fire, too. We wanted peace, all right. We wanted to live.

After the firefight in the Circle of Sorrow, we reaffirmed our commitment to peace and the killing of dinks, and we tried to puzzle out what in the hell had happened there. How many had we been up against? A reinforced company? A battalion?

"G-2 says maybe no more than a platoon or two," said Tender.

"Balls," said Thompson.

"You lie," said Jones.

We complained about how long the ARVN took getting there. We praised God for the Phantom pilots who brought in the heat. Jones said the fortifications we had seen in the Circle were nothing compared with what they had at their headquarters across the border in Cambodia. We all agreed: It was better they had set up camp in Cambodia rather than on this side of the border, otherwise some sorry-assed general would be getting ideas.

Division was happy with the body count in the Circle of Sorrow. It liked all the rifles that turned up in the cache the dinks were defending. Brigade was happy that Division was happy. And I was happiest of all. We had bought ourselves a few days of standdown, and that brought my calendar right up to R and R.

"Short!" I said when the LT told us.

"You going to be in Saigon?" Neumann asked.

"Sure," I said. "The LT's giving me one extra night to take in the sights."

"Do me a favor?"

"Anything."

"There's a woman I'd like you to see. She's

Vietnamese. I knew her there. When I transferred to the Cav, I didn't get back to her to explain. She's a good woman. She deserves to know that I'm not coming back."

"She really loved this guy," said Jackpot. "He makes it look so easy."

"Shitty favor," I said.

"Forget it then," Neumann said.

"Maybe you'll get to Saigon again yourself."

"By then it wouldn't be the same with us. She would want it to be, but it wouldn't. It's something better taken care of now."

"But not by you," I said.

"That's right," he said. "That's the way it plays."

"I'll do it," I said.

"Maybe you'll like her," said Jackpot.

There were times when you thought a lot about women and times when you did not have it in you to think about them at all. When the guns stopped and the wind whispered that you were still alive, it was a woman's sound. But when you remembered it later, dreamed it again, the cackling of incoming bullets, the thundering questions asked by the shells, it drove off every desire you had. There were days when you could not keep your eyes off the Vietnamese girls, wanting them. And there were other days when wanting them made you turn your eyes away.

They were so sad and beautiful. They learned too much too soon. What you were discovering at nineteen or twenty-two, they had learned at their mothers' breasts. A mother's song is slow and plaintive; she suckled soldiers and their widows and whores.

You compared them with the women back in

the World. And you felt that you were too old for the girls of your past, much too old. Maybe, you thought, you could get younger again, later. But for this one year at least you were way out beyond them.

Neumann's girl back home was named Donna Jarret, and she wrote him regularly. She even sent me a letter after she learned from him that I was alone. I believe he cared about her, cared about the girl in Saigon, cared about Tuyet. But did that make him better or worse than the others? I don't know.

The others certainly did not complicate things with caring. Jones favored a blow bath just beyond the wire. Diaz and Thompson sought the pleasure of an itinerant whore somebody had named Tricia. And Jackpot was after the sweetest of them all, the shy hootchmaid we called Co. Co was their word for Miss, and we called her that because she yielded nothing, not even her name. Still, Jackpot lavished trinkets on her, tried to make conversation, teased. She remained coy and silent. Secretly, I was rooting for her.

The day before I was due to go on R and R, Jackpot stayed in the rack while the rest of us went to chow. I happened back to the hootch later to pick up something I'd forgotten, and I was sorry to find him in his final assault.

Co's blouse was open, her bra unsnapped and loose up around her neck. Her black silk pants were twisted at her ankles, and Jackpot was awkwardly trying to find a way between her hobbled legs. Co squirmed but did not make a sound. Jackpot found his mark and struggled to make a rhythm without her help. She turned her face to where I stood in the doorway. Her eyes were open, her mouth lightly shut. She looked at me with a face like a sigh.

Jackpot came loudly and then rolled off her. She sat up, buttoned her blouse without fixing the bra, pulled up her pants, then reached for Jackpot's fatigues, which were sprawled next to the bunk. In an instant she had his wallet, and she ran past me out of the hootch.

"She's got your money," I said.

"No sweat," said Jackpot, a silly smile on his face. "Hell, if I'd of known that was all it took to get a shot of leg, I'd of had her a long time ago."

I reached Saigon late the next afternoon and didn't have to report to Camp Alpha at Tan Son Nhut Air Base until the next afternoon, so I caught a tiny blue and yellow taxi right outside the main gate and showed the driver the address Neumann had given me.

"Three hundred p," he said, grinning gold.

"You take army money or only piasters?" I said.

His smile got broader.

"Three dollar MPC," he said. It was a swindle. Military Pay Currency went for three times that on the black market. But I nodded, and we eased between two Hondas into the traffic.

A sign at the gate said WARNING: YOU ARE ABOUT TO ENTER ONE OF THE MOST DANGEROUS COMBAT AREAS IN VIETNAM. A PUBLIC HIGHWAY. PLEASE DRIVE CARE-FULLY. It turned out to be a masterpiece of under-statement. The traffic was jammed, but the jam moved along at about forty miles an hour. Motorscooters, jeeps, three-wheeled pedal cabs, cyclos, oxcarts, all swirled in and out of one another's paths. We turned about in front of a roaring, oblivious deuce and a half and made off in the opposite direction.

"No rush," I said.

"No sweat," said the driver.

He weaved in and out of side streets, past barbed wire and guard posts. I was bewildered by the swarming crowds, the size of the buildings. The treelined boulevards were shady and beautiful, until you came to the barricades. There was even a large brick cathedral, and across from it a teeming black market in drugs.

The driver pulled up abruptly in front of a faded yellow office. I paid him and went upstairs to the floor where Neumann's Vietnamese girlfriend was supposed to work. The office was a single big room, empty in the center. Awkward, off-balance old desks bordered the walls under shelves piled high with letter boxes of pen-speckled cardboard. One large fan swept slowly overhead, not cooling, just gently blending the perfume, sweat and burnt-rubber smoke from French cigarettes.

The girl nearest the door finally looked up at me. She seemed surprised. I had cleaned up as best I could, but I was still definitely a grunt. And I was out of place.

"May I help you?" she asked, standing at her chair. She was small and very fragile. She wore a white lace Ao Dai and black silk pants. Her shiny black hair reached her waist. Her wrists were as delicate as the easiest vine.

127

I pulled out the paper Neumann had given me with the name.

"I'm looking for Miss Nguyen Ba Thi," I said, pronouncing it Noo-yen.

She blushed.

"I am Nguyen Ba Thi," she said. She pronounced it Nwin.

"Jim Neumann asked me to come and see you. I am an old friend of his. We are in the same unit."

I found myself speaking very slowly, as if to give her time to translate.

"Please come back in one hour and fifteen minutes," she said. Her English was as good as my own.

As I left the building, I tried to orient myself so I could find my way back. But I quickly became lost in the swarms of Vietnamese on the twisting streets. Vendors shouted at me. Little boys tugged on my sleeves offering black-market piasters, dope and virgin sisters. The crowd squeezed, carrying me toward a dark doorway. As it swept me in, I twisted free and ran into the street. My chest heaved. Taxis honked and slammed on their brakes. I crouched, waiting for the first shots.

They did not come. Inside the doorway was an arcade. Custom tailors, ladies' garments. Stands selling toiletries and photographic film.

I was ashamed of how afraid I had been. But until then the only time I had come into contact with Vietnamese was under the cover of our guns. We had only two categories: They were either our Vietnamese or their Vietnamese, and since we could not always tell the difference, we relied upon superior force. At Ouan Loi we let a few in to wash our clothes, make our bunks, scrub our pots and satisfy our itches. In the bush they huddled together against us. But in Saigon for the first time I saw them as a nation, and I could not imagine them not meaning me harm.

Up Le Loi Street stood the white National Assembly building. To its right on Tu Do, the bar girls worked out of places named Rose Petal, New York, the Mod. To its left stood the Hotel Continental, a clean stucco place with a veranda bar. I decided to treat myself to a drink. Gin and tonic would have been most appropriate. Or vermouth cassis. I drank bourbon instead. They had every possible brand.

Thi was waiting at the door of her office building when I returned. She held a parasol against the waning afternoon sun. Surely the sun could not have been too strong for her. It could have been that she carried it for fashion. But I prefer to think she was simply more subtle than we are. We never seek the shade until we are burned.

"We shall take different taxis," she said as she handed me a small calling card bearing an address.

"Where are we going?"

"My home."

"You don't need to invite me home, really," I said. "Maybe we could just have coffee somewhere nearby."

"Please come to my home," she said, and went to the curb to get a cab. She found one and got me inside it, giving the driver directions. As I left, she was hailing another for herself.

My driver turned through a series of progressively narrower and more chaotic streets until he pulled up at what appeared to be a tailor shop. I got out and paid him in piasters I had changed for MPC with a streetboy. When the taxi drove off, Thi emerged from a doorway next to the store.

"Please follow me," she said, and we started upstairs.

A gaggle of youngsters screamed down the stairwell. They ran past us, almost knocking me off-balance. Thi got to the top landing and opened a door as I made my way up the narrow last flight.

The living room was furnished sparely—a small bed, an insubstantial chair, a wooden chest, some mats and pillows on the floor. She walked in first. I leaned down awkwardly to remove my muddy boots. She looked at my pants tied off at the ankles. My socks had a number of holes. She smiled.

I would not have had her so decent. She probably expected a kind word from Neumann, I thought, a promise about the future. I brought neither. To make up a hopeful story would have been cruel. The best I could do was to hurt her and go.

Thi came from the kitchen with a pot of tea and two cups. I thanked her as she sat down across from me on a mat.

"What does Jim say?" she finally asked.

"Why did we take two taxis?"

"He asked that?"

"I was just wondering."

"Because some people, some police, do not like Vietnamese women with American soldiers. Sometimes they make trouble."

"Jim is well," I said. "He sends his love."

She blushed and made me regret even this little lie.

"But he asked me to tell you that he thinks he won't be able to get back to Saigon to see you. We are far off up north near Cambodia."

"He will never come?" She asked it curiously, without a trace of bitterness.

"He cannot get here from where we are."

Thi poured me some more tea.

"And how did you come?" she asked. There was no disbelief in it. She was not debating me. She just wanted to understand.

"I am on my way to Tokyo," I said. "I leave tomorrow."

"Leave Vietnam forever?"

"Just a week. Like a holiday."

"R and R," she said. "Then maybe Jim will come to Saigon on R and R, too. You will have dinner with me here?"

"Oh, no. But thank you. You don't have to entertain me. Really. I just came to deliver the message from Jim. I'll go now if you tell me how to get back downtown."

I sat dumbly for a moment, feeling clumsy and a little irritated at how well she was taking it. She said nothing, but I could tell it would offend her if I left. So I finally agreed to stay.

"If you are tired," she said, "lie down and rest while I make our dinner."

I did and fell asleep in an instant. She woke me later with a gentle tap on the shoulder that was like a low branch brushing against me in the breeze.

"I have made French dishes," she said. "When I came to Saigon, it was a French city."

We ate chicken and sauce, Dalat lettuce salad, peas and almonds and tropical fruit. We drank an

Algerian wine that on my Kool-Aid palate tasted as superb as a fine vintage château. We drank absinthe after dinner. I complimented her. She smiled. As soon as I finished the last of the strong, milky liquor, I stood up and bowed a little at the waist.

"Thi, thank you very much. Please let me pay, at least for the wine."

"It is not good," she said as I reached for my wallet.

"I must leave now and look for a hotel before curfew," I said. My uneasiness with her was gone, and I was smiling at last.

"Where do you stay?"

"I'll find a place."

"You have none?"

"Not yet."

"You will stay here then. Tomorrow I do not work. We will have breakfast. We will talk some more."

"I can't, Thi. I'd better leave now."

"You are not like Jim. You are a little afraid. I want you to stay. I always sleep on the mat anyway. I was a child in the hamlets, and I have never enjoyed the softness of a bed. Please stay."

The problem was the absinthe. Thi's beauty. The fear subsiding and the memory of the fear. These things pushed me away and pulled me back. We were temporary men, short-timers all. The best of their own were far away or dead. And here I was with a wallet full of piasters and MPC, a head of steam from the alcohol and a ticket out. We came and we left, and there was never enough time to close the distance between us. We were hope, but hope was vain. They were vulnerable, too vulnerable, and it was wrong to take advantage of them.

"Please do not feel you would impose," she said. "I like to talk to you."

I was weak. Maybe I wanted a piece of that hope, too. I gave in.

We talked about Saigon and traded our histories. She told me she had been raised in the Mekong Delta as a young girl but had moved north to stay with an uncle in Saigon when she was six. Her mother had been killed by terrorists and her father conscripted by the government. Her uncle became wealthy and sent her to school until she was eighteen. Then she took a job with the Ministry of Information. She read American newspapers for a living.

I told her I had grown up near Chicago, and I drew a rough map of the World to show her. I said Illinois was flat farmland like the Mekong Delta and that Chicago was America's Can Tho. I'm sure she knew all that, but she listened anyway. I told her I had gone through parochial school and public high school there. Then on to college and the draft.

It was starting to get dark, so Thi laid out her mat. I cleaned up a little in the bathroom. When I returned, she had lighted three candles before a small shrine by the window. They set the room in dusky light and made the shadows move. Thi left the room and I took off my fatigue shirt and socks. My feet were dirty. I hid them under the covers. I wore my pants because I didn't have on any underwear. In the jungle underwear just meant more heat and chafing. This wasn't the jungle.

"Good night, Thi," I said when she came back in a long silk robe. "Thank you very much." I turned to my stomach. Thi sat on the mat and arranged a pillow.

I had almost dozed off when I felt Thi's weight on the bed beside me. She rubbed my neck softly. I looked up at her. The wavering ceremonial light played across her breasts where the robe had fallen open. I looked at her face. She was smiling. She bent down and kissed me, and in one movement she brought herself on top of me. The robe hissed silk as it covered us both. My hands found the small of her back. She was so light, hardly more than a touch. The touch moved. She kissed my lips and breathed near my ear. My hands moved to her breasts.

I rolled away and sat up on the edge of the bed, my head pounding. I took one long breath and turned to her.

"I want you, Thi. Believe that I want you. But it isn't good. I'm a grunt. I'm an American. I'm another Neumann. In twenty hours I'll be gone for good."

"I understand," she said. "I should not have tried. I am sorry."

"Don't be sorry. For godsake don't be sorry." I kissed her, and she touched my cheek with another offer. I pulled away.

Thi moved off the bed and back to the mat. I sat, face turned away from her, trying not to shudder.

"Thank you," Thi said, and she lay down and slept.

But I could not calm down. I got up and walked to her twice during the night but backed away both times. She was deep asleep, and that was lucky. I would have seemed so ludicrous to her, so impotent. I finally dropped off just before dawn and awakened only to her kiss. Now it seems that I never awakened at all but only dreamed that gentle touch. The quiet breakfast. Thi's kindness. Her laughter. Our long embrace when I left.

I thought of her the next day on the airplane to Tokyo. I thought of Sharon and Donna Jarret, too. All the broken connections.

# 4

# Xuan The

Jackpot died while I was away. That was the first thing Neumann told me when I came off R and R. He had taken an AK round as he left the chopper on a dusk assault. It had happened the evening I was in Saigon. I made Neumann be sure about the day, the time. It was important because at precisely that moment I had been with Thi, drinking in her beauty, talking about the World. Jackpot bled to death slowly. The Dustoffs couldn't land. Thi's breasts moved freely under the silk, under my palm. Jackpot's blood is dark on the shadowy grass of the LZ. Thi's lips are dark in the flickering candlelight. The blood beads like dew on the leaves.

"What kind of crazy-ass motherfucker are you?" said Jones.

"Bad sense of humor, man," said Diaz.

Bones just shook his head and spat through the doorway into the dirt.

"Look," I said. "I'm sorry. It makes me feel

strange, too. Like maybe it wouldn't have happened if I hadn't gone slack. Like it all should have been the other way around."

"Maybe it should have," said Thompson, and they all followed him out of the hootch.

I stopped Neumann as he left.

"You understand," I said.

"Better save the Tristan shit for back in the World," he said.

But that wasn't it. I wasn't looking for the ecstasy of death. I just wanted the dull pulse of survival, the sense of connection with the future. I had not sought even that much with Thi. But still, death had stalked me there. It was death that had embraced me. This was what chilled me so.

"I wasn't trying to be smart," I said.

"You weren't succeeding either," said Neumann.

Jackpot's death brought another lull. That made everyone feel lousy. Then the lull lengthened and we began to think it was mortgaging somebody else's future. There were missions now and then, but nobody even spat at us. Then Angelo got hit through the calf. It was a fluke. A kid popped out of a spider hole and got off one shot. He turned out to be a young kid, maybe fifteen, when we killed him.

Angelo's wound wasn't serious. They dusted him off, but only as far as Quan Loi. If the bullet had clipped a bone, he would have gone home. But this way it did not even count, for him or for us. We visited him every evening in the little hospital, talked it all out and decided it was a rotten deal of the cards.

After Angelo's wound, things got even more ominous. No mortar attacks, no contact. The LT said that by the usual cycle of things it should have been an active time. The dinks, he said, usually infiltrated a lot of troops and laid in a lot of supplies this time of year, and that meant you were bound to stumble on them. But day after day, nothing but signs that didn't pan out. The bats flew away one night, but the next day nobody died in our sector. Then the flame trees blossomed when they shouldn't have, but still nothing. The intelligence officers ground out predictions of high points in enemy activity. Rumor elevated these to impending ground probes, rocket barrages. We got so that we hoped for them. Anything to break the silence. But nothing happened.

The ledger was going way out of balance, and it scared us. Jones thought the dinks must have been putting in caches across the border for a big push later. Thompson disagreed. He thought we were winning the war at last. But he did not like it much. Bad for the nerves. Tender listened to his radio and had no opinion at all. And as for Diaz, he groped toward a new myth.

"Jackpot died for us," he said, and we all hated the idea, knowing that it was true.

Meanwhile, Neumann was becoming withdrawn and secretive. He still played his music, but it had gone abstract, remote. Jones thought he was mourning Jackpot, and he dug the new sound. I wanted to talk out the thing about Thi. I wanted to explain that it wasn't what he thought. But I was afraid to bring it up.

And then we started to see him holding animated conversations with the LT. They went to the battalion TOC together many afternoons. They began to butter up the supply stiffs but never came back with anything they'd scrounged. One day, both of them flew off in the colonel's bird. Nobody knew where.

"You can be sure of one thing," said Angelo, his leg strung up in a canvas noose at the end of the hospital bed. "They ain't asking a grunt's opinion. Only thing a colonel ever asked me is where's my hometown."

Finally, Neumann let me in on it. He was planning a new operation, but it was not combat. The Blues, he told me, were going to adopt a village.

The lull showed no sign of abating, he said. Morale was slipping. Our habits were becoming sloppy. We got ripped too early, stayed stoned too late. When we did have a mission, we were getting to be as rag-tag as the ARVN. We had to have something definite to do or we'd fall completely apart. So Neumann wanted us to go on a goodwill mission. We could make a difference in a few people's lives, he said. We could do something for them they could not do for themselves. We could build.

I told him what I thought about that. I told him it was stupid, vain. The most we could ever do for these people was to discipline our fire. The rest was hopeless. But this only encouraged him. It was, I think, the very immensity of the sadness that spurred him on. He would save them, no matter what the odds. And he saw no conflict between the things the Blues had been doing and the things he wanted them to do. He refused to draw a line between war and peace.

"Not everyone can do both at once," I said.

"They're both the same," he said, "the two sides of it."

"It will put Thompson right over the brink."

"He wouldn't go. It's all set up. He'll be promoted, and he'll substitute for me with the unit when I go to Xuan The."

"Xuan The?"

"The ville," he said. "Morgan, I need your help. Don't fight me on this."

"Who's fighting?" I said. "It's a lull."

He stuck out his hand and, shaking mine, looped his other arm around my shoulders the way an alderman might.

"Look at it this way," he said, moving us toward the LT's hootch where he was about to volunteer my help in persuading the others. "It's a way to learn a trade."

Neumann mentioned the firefight by the broken bridge when he explained his idea to the Blues, but only by way of placing Xuan The. No one said anything about the man he had killed there. Neumann had his secret reasons, and these reasons had their own secrets, and we honored them all.

He told the Blues that Xuan The was the perfect place because of Apache, our Vietnamese Kit Carson scout. It had been his home. We trusted him, and working in the ville would be a way of showing it. After all, he was one of our Vietnamese, one of our very best. He had had his apostasy, of course, but that was long ago. As a young man

Apache had been cashiered into the Viet Minh. Later, when the Americans started to arrive, he surrendered and offered his services. He liked Americans, he said.

Apache did not talk much about himself. He had a little hootch out near the wire where he tended a garden and entertained the mama-sans at lunchtime like a son. You see, what made him such a good Vietnamese was that when we did not want him, he was very nearly invisible. And in his way, he was absolutely honest.

"Is that man telling the truth?" we would ask him of a suspected Viet Cong.

"Vietnamese never tell truth," he would say, his lips pulling back slowly to reveal a broad, paradoxical, Asian smile.

"There it is," we would say. "There it is."

So I had to go elsewhere to find out more about Xuan The. None of the grunts who passed through Quan Loi seemed to know anything about it, which was a good sign. You only really remembered the killing ground. The chopper pilots knew it as a place on the map, a landmark they wheeled around when they were on their way to someplace else. Finally, I took a walk over to brigade headquarters and talked to a major who seemed to know the score. He was the staff officer charged with pacification in our sector. It was the kind of job majors always got, the kind that made them so unpleasant.

"Apache was pretty unclear just what kind of place it is," I said.

"Exactly," he said. "They always are. That's why you have to have objective indicators. Facts, son, facts."

"Numbers," I said.

"Roger that," he said. "Number of mortar rounds going in. Number of rounds coming out. Number of recruitment potential, male. Number of recruitment potential, female."

"Pardon?"

"The Cong, son. Who they can grab off. All the data."

"What do the numbers add up to?" I asked.

"A grade."

"You give the Vietnamese grades?"

"Not your individual Viet," he said. "We do it by the ville. A, B, C, and so on. Xuan The is a B minus. Plenty of room for improvement."

"What do the grades measure?"

"Friendship," he said. "By the numbers."

We grunts had a different system. Sure, it was hard to tell our dinks from theirs, but we had a general rule. Ordinarily speaking, our dinks were the ones who stayed put when they saw us. Their dinks were the ones who ran away. Friendship.

The people in Xuan The, of course, did not run away. Apache had gotten the whole thing set up before the first contingent of Blues arrived. Neumann had been scrounging building materials for weeks, and by the time we moved into the ville he had an intricate supply network set up. He wanted to start by rebuilding a crude dispensary that had fallen to air strikes years before. The French had built it in the early 1950's, but it lay in ruins overgrown with vines. The dispensary had once served Xuan The and half a dozen communities nearby. Neumann hoped it could be used as a base for stepped-up medical-aid missions in the sector.

I went with him on his second trip to Xuan The. We drove there after breakfast. It was still quite cool, but the sharp, sweet smell of rotting plants and the fecal stink of the paddies mixed with the stinging odor of cooking fish and made the air thick and close. The single passable road into Xuan The came up from the south and stretched along a deep jungle that formed the eastern border of the town. The road clogged with mud during the wet season, sometimes so badly that even a jeep couldn't get through. But during the dry season it was big enough and had a firm enough bed to carry a deuce-and-a-half truck or a Sheridan tank.

About a dozen kids met us as we bumped into town. They pushed up against the jeep when it stopped. One boy grabbed at the hair on my arm. To the smooth-skinned Vietnamese, we hirsute Americans must have seemed halfway between man and beast.

"*Di di mau,*" Apache barked, and the children backed off just enough to let us out of the vehicle.

Neumann pulled out a handful of candy, threw it in the air and watched the kids scramble for their share. One tiny girl, no older than three, stood near the edge of the road. She had been hanging on to her older brother until he joined the fight for the chocolate. Deserted now and too young to join in the tussle, she stood awkwardly in the short grass with tears blossoming in her eyes. Neumann walked up to her, unwrapped a piece of candy and held it out. She did not budge. Neumann moved the candy right under her nose to give her a whiff of its sweetness. Without a change of expression, the little girl reached up a clumsy hand, took the confection and began to lick it sadly. Neumann looked toward me, shrugged his shoulders and laughed.

North of the cleared space that held the bamboo and thatch hootches ran a small creek where the villagers washed, bathed and got water for irrigation. The paddies, stream and treeline formed a triangle. The hootches roughly followed the sides of the triangle, one deep, and in the center of the cleared space there was a primitive gazebo, its thatched roof supported by eight thick bamboo poles. The whole town leaned slightly toward the creek, so that even during the rains it stayed reasonably dry.

We walked down the dusty path past the hootches to the ruins. Vietnamese men and women peeked furtively out of the doorways at us, then darted back into the shadows. Their children bounded around us as Neumann asked Apache to summon the townspeople to help us clear the building site.

Most of the villagers were available to work. Dry season meant no rice crops to tend. The men and women came to the ruins slowly, tentatively, wiser than their children who danced and played heedlessly around us, grabbing at our hair and toying with the butts of the rifles slung from our shoulders.

"Tell them we are here to start building the dispensary," Neumann told Apache. "Tell them that the first thing we must do is to clear up the rubble and save what we can. We will form two groups and work in shifts. We will save all the concrete block and bricks, piling them over there. The badly broken things and the rest we will pile back there under the trees."

The people listened quietly as Apache translated. The men had all taken off their hats when Neumann began to speak, and they held them with both hands in front of them like mourners. Their faces were as hard and dark as aged wood. They wore simple, loose clothes that hid the wanness of their bodies. Death staked its claim upon these rural people early, invading their eyes and tormenting their skin with its promise. When Apache pointed, they looked in unison toward the rubble.

The French had built the dispensary near a thick grove of trees to take advantage of the shade. Half of one wall remained standing, waist high, but the forest curled its tendrils around the concrete blocks. A thick root threatened to crack the base of the wall. We would have to sever the root to protect the foundation. The remains of the rest of the walls lay scattered in piles. Twisted tin fragments from the roof poked up here and there. Whatever wood hadn't been splintered useless had rotted gray. A brilliant blue-blossomed vine spread over the whole pile like fingers settling papers in a breeze.

When Apache finished, Neumann walked to the rubble and started to work alone. He was to take the first shift. I leaned up against a tree and sipped water from my canteen. The Vietnamese just stood nearby at first as Neumann began to pick up large chunks of brick and rock and carry them to the two locations he had described. Neumann worked on, and after several minutes the men and women slowly began to move about, hesitantly trying the chunks with their feet. Sweat rolled off Neumann's face and spread dark wings across the back and shoulders of his fatigues. The villagers caught his rhythm and began to haul the rocks with something close to enthusiasm.

Long years of war and the cruelty of nature in the tropics had taught the rural Vietnamese something: One thing was as good as the next, or as bad. War, peace; rain, sun; American, French. Same-same. Yin and yang. But here at work with this sweaty American, this big, blond-headed man with a thick moustache and bright blue eyes, they seemed to acknowledge a new purpose. An elderly worker tapped Neumann on the shoulder and pointed to a broken brick on the ground. Neumann screwed up his eyes, pulled at his chin theatrically and pointed to the scrap pile. The old man bowed.

Meanwhile, I noticed that someone in the distance was watching Neumann very closely. I did not pay much attention until after I had taken my turn at the wreckage. She stood off near one of the hootches, tending an urn of water. I guess she was about nineteen years old. She stood little more than five feet tall and had that look that young Vietnamese peasant girls have—grace even in rags. She wore a white cotton blouse that hung gently like a curtain from her breasts. It was not tucked into her black pants, so that when she bent over to get a ladle of water I caught a glimpse of the soft olive skin of her back. She watched him closely, and she came to something near a smile whenever he happened to glance her way.

She already liked Neumann too much, I thought,

but I could understand why. He was as big as any two of the villagers. By noon he had taken off his shirt, and his strong back glistened with sweat. Why should she have been immune to the field of force everyone else felt when they were near him? Before we left the ville, I asked Apache her name.

"Tuyet," he said. "Le Van Tuyet. She is daughter of my friend who is dead. VC kill my friend. They kidnap her brother. She will like Sergeant Neumann boo-coo."

"What do you think about that, Apache?"

He just looked at me as if I had asked him to comment on the presidency of Richard Nixon or the behavior of the rains or anything else he could not hope to change.

After we got the wreckage nearly cleared away, Neumann paced off the size of the uncovered foundation. The French had built the original dispensary strong, and the foundation proved still to be good. Neumann counted the salvageable blocks and bricks and had a short conversation with the village elders through Apache.

I went to the jeep, slouched down behind the wheel and watched Tuyet standing in her doorway and concentrating on Neumann. Her face, even from that distance, told me everything. But still I had the foolish hope that Neumann might never notice her and that she would be too diffident to seek him out.

It was quite a while before I spent another day in Xuan The. The LT wouldn't spring me loose. Said he didn't like losing both Neumann and me at the same time. I couldn't see what difference it made.

Things had gone so slack they had us pulling security on convoys like a bunch of MPs.

The red dust exploded behind the deuce and a halfs, billowing up in our faces, sandblasting our eyes. We wore our bandanas in triangles over our noses like highwaymen. Two by two, spaced out the length of the convoy, we rode in jeeps mounted with machine guns. One trip out, one trip back. Day after day.

When a convoy safely reached the main highway, we would peel off and the MPs would take over. Then we would turn around and wait for the next trucks inbound. The boys of the Coca-Cola brigade caught on immediately, and they would be waiting there with soda and ice for fifty cents MPC. The LT brought along a few gallons of water in big cans so we could slosh the grime out of our mouths and off our faces as soon as the dust settled. But the boys still did a brisk business.

"Where's your older brother, dink?" Thompson demanded as he paid the cola boy for another bottle. "Don't forget to gimme change."

"No change," said the boy, darting out of Thompson's reach. "No change. Same-same. No brother."

"No shit," said Thompson.

"They just so afraid of you, redneck, that all the older brothers have skeedaddled all the way back to Hanoi," said Bones.

"Well, they sure as hell ain't afraid of you," Thompson said. "Now you *know* I ain't calling you a pussy, which you ain't. But you sure ain't exactly lethal either, if you know what I mean."

"No guns for me, redneck," he said, and then

he repeated the phrase that gave him his name. "Like I told the draft board, it's just something I feel in my bones."

He was the only man in the Blues, save Thompson, who never went to Xuan The. Neumann often asked him to, and the LT would have agreed to let him now and again. But Bones always declined. He said he didn't feel right about leaving the others. Something was bound to happen if he did. Somebody would die. But that was not the only reason.

Bones was a CO, noncombatant. He wouldn't even hump M-60 belts in a pinch. But he made up for that by carrying a regular intensive-care unit around with him. Extra morphine, chrome instruments, stainless-steel scalpels, anything he could scrounge that could ease our pain or save our lives. What Bones had seen in the bush had scraped his conscience pretty thin, but he only slipped once that I know of. It was in the Circle of Sorrow. A man lay moaning about twenty meters in front of our position. The dinks' machine guns mowed back and forth. Bones started to move up anyway, dragging the smallest of his medic's bags with him, the one with the holy water. He crawled very slowly, trying not to attract the dinks' attention. As he approached, the crying man's body began to twitch frantically and the moaning stopped. The dink machine-gunner was pouring rounds into it. Ten, twenty, fifty rounds, tattering the corpse, sending bits of flesh into the air. Finally, the gunman stopped. Bones waited for a moment and then continued to move up to what was left of the dead man. When he reached it, he put his hand under the corpse and found what he wanted. Three of them. Suddenly, he was on one knee, hurling the grenades toward the enemy bunker. One, two . . . three. The last one he aimed for the gunport. It missed.

He never did say anything about it, and neither did we. But I guess what Bones did in the Circle of Sorrow reminded all of us for just a moment that even in that shitty episode of our shitty little 365-day war, there might have been more to a man than whether he lived or died.

"Come on, Bones," said Diaz. "Come on out to the ville with us. The dispensary is going along real fine. And that's right up your alley. Medicine and all. It's better than this silly shit."

"None of my affair," said Bones.

"It helps people."

"Doesn't everything?" said Bones.

That took Diaz back for a moment. But he pressed on.

"What's wrong with giving people a hand?" he asked.

"Nothing."

"Ask the LT. He'll tell you it's OK."

"I'm sure he would."

"There's no shooting," said Diaz. "It's real peaceful."

"Sure."

"Then come on just once."

"I don't want to get involved."

"That don't make sense," said Diaz. "You'd put your ass on the line any time for one of us. That's as involved as you can get."

"It's different."

"Different?" said Diaz. "How?"

The LT sat on the bumper of the jeep, leaning his elbows on his knees and spitting a tight shot pattern into the dust.

"Bones is right," he said. "It's all in the way you look at it."

"But what's wrong with Xuan The?" Diaz asked.

The LT sat up, threw his shoulders back and stretched. He looked stiff and tired. He showed his age.

"It's all right by me," he said, "because it's all right by the colonel. And it's all right by him because it's all right by the general."

The LT stood up and scratched.

"But it definitely is part of the war," he said, and then he broke into a big, stupid grin. "Grab 'em by the hearts and minds, and their balls will follow."

"Balls ain't what Neumann's grabbing," said Thompson.

"Tuyet sure is fine all right," said Reed. "Mighty fine."

"What's she like?" I asked.

"She don't say much," said Jones. "That's her strongest quality. She could even get along with Tender."

"I like her," said Tender.

"Shit," said Jones, picking the stones out of his sole with a knife. "What you know about it? Nobody know who these people are. Nothin' there to like or not like. Just a great big question. Nobody know what goes on behind them slope eyes."

"Can't fuck worth a damn," said Thompson. "Just lie there like a bag of warm shit."

"Then why you pay that pig Tricia?" said Jones.

"Why spend money to buy what you could get free from your own asshole?"

"He don't reach," said Reed.

And we all laughed so hard you'd have thought the dust was dope.

"They any others there worth the screwing?" said Thompson.

"Look at him," said Jones. "He all of a sudden got a big six-inch interest in pacification."

"Maybe Neumann wasn't so dumb after all," said Thompson. "That's all I'm thinkin'."

"That isn't it," said Tender.

"Spit it out," said Jones.

Tender turned aside. His fingers fiddled with the silent radio handset.

"Tender just means Neumann don't care especially about the girl," said Diaz. "You've all been there. You know what I'm talking about. Neumann really digs the ville. That's what he cares about."

"Tuyet means something special to him, too," said Tender.

"I think maybe she does," I said.

"Come on," said Jones. "She just another dink. She don't even know the words."

"Hopeless," I said. "That's what interests him."

"Shit," said Jones.

Then we heard the low rumble that meant we were about to move out again. In the distance the big gray wake of a convoy rose above the road like smoke from a napalm strike.

"Wet 'em down," said the LT. And we lined up to soak our bandanas and get ourselves up again as thieves.

"Morgan," said the LT. "If you want to go out to Xuan The and have a look, it's OK. See for yourself."

"See what?"

"That Neumann is doing all right," he said.

The day I finally drove out with Neumann again, Tuyet was standing at the edge of the ville waiting for us.

"*Chao*, Jim," she said, smiling so broadly that it almost marred her beauty.

"*Chao co*," he said. "Bill, this is Tuyet." And then he touched her hair lightly. I nodded to her as Neumann invited me to join him in Tuyet's hootch for some tea.

A cooking fire lighted the shadowy interior of the hootch in flickering red. A pan of water boiled on the fire, and the fishy smell of breakfast filled the cool room. Tuyet's mother sat near the doorway in the rectangle of morning light. She kneaded a rice paste in a flat pan and said something in Vietnamese to Tuyet's baby brother. He left for a moment. The mama-san's arms were thin and sinewy as she worked the dough. She could not have been more than forty years old, but her face was stretched tight on the bone, giving it the look of a skull. Tuyet's baby brother toddled back in. He was lighter-skinned, almost white, and his features were heavier than Tuyet's. For a moment I saw in the little boy's face the leer of an American soldier long since gone away.

The room was bare: sleeping mats rolled up and stowed along the walls, a wooden crate in the center of the dirt floor serving as a table. In a corner near me sat the yoke and trays they used for heavy loads and a large wicker pot. I leaned against one of the poles that supported the woven walls, drawing up my legs Indian-style under me. Tuyet lighted a stick of incense and put it smoldering into an empty C-ration can. On one wall hung a gaudy red Tet calendar marking the day in Vietnamese, Chinese, French and English. In a far corner, near one of the mat rolls, lay Neumann's silver flute, uncased and shining.

We had our tea in silence. Then Neumann led me through the ville on the way to the building site. The Vietnamese hung back in the smoky shadows just inside the doors of their hootches as we passed. Neumann strode by, not even noticing how they watched him. How many little villes like this had he and I passed through? You paid no attention to anything but what harm they might have been hiding. You searched their bunkers and looked for young men. You half-expected somebody to leap out of a spider hole and lob a grenade. And sometimes you got what you expected.

But here Neumann walked as easily as if it had been his own hometown. And I noticed things I had never paid attention to before. How tiny the children were, how thin the walls of straw. How little the people spoke with one another, how careful they were to stay out of our way.

The dispensary walls had risen to shoulder-high all around. Neumann had managed to scrounge a good deal of cement block, so he could afford to throw away all but the least damaged salvage. The growing structure looked strong and angular against the dark, formless threat of the jungle. In a way, it made the jungle seem even more ominous, just as

Neumann's presence in the ville made it seem more alien.

"OK. OK. OK," said the four men detailed to help work that day. Apache introduced them. Each bowed slightly at the sound of his name. I bowed back. Neumann leaned up against the wall and smiled at all the formality.

"Am I doing this right?" I asked.

"You worry too much," he said. "Just be sure to set the bricks straight."

"Looks like you're building this to last forever," I said.

"They'll be here that long," he said as he began to unload the supplies from the back of the jeep.

"Can they understand you?" I asked.

One of the Vietnamese caught my eye and bowed again.

"Only through Apache," said Neumann. "Jones tried to teach a few of them the vocabulary of soul, but they didn't seem too interested."

"What about the girl?"

"She likes the music," he said. "It's a kind of language, too, you know. We have others."

By the time we got the mortar mixed and the blocks lined up, the sun was high in the sky and the shadows short, hunched spots beneath our feet. The Vietnamese knew their jobs well. Neumann had to show me what to do, but after a while even I got the hang of it. It was easy to see why the Blues liked coming to Xuan The for what they called Good Dink Duty. It was hard work, but you were on your own. No hassles. And when you stepped back a few paces, you could see what you had accomplished.

After a couple of hours in the sun we had to find some shade and take some water and salt. Tuyet brought us the water cans and then went back to heat us some rations for lunch.

"What happens to the girl when you leave?" I asked.

"Don't worry," he said. "You won't have to come here and explain."

"I don't know whether she's as strong as Thi. She's so very young. What if there's a child?"

"Watch me, old friend," he said. "This time I might really surprise you."

"You're a constant source of astonishment," I said, and let it pass.

In the afternoon Neumann worked for a few hours, then made sure I knew what I was doing before he went off to take a break with Tuyet. For a while I could hear the soft jazz coming from inside her hootch. No longer abstract and distant, the music was simple again, direct. Eventually it stopped, and the only sound was the click and scrape of brick against brick and the snicker of the wind high in the trees.

Once the work on the dispensary was well under way, Neumann began brooding over bigger plans for Xuan The. As a first step he wanted to set up a work schedule dividing the labor among the paddies, the construction and the routine chores of maintenance. At first the village elders resisted. Division of labor was not part of their tradition. They had only one organizing principle: the seasons. The whole village planted and harvested their crops to the timing of the rains. For as long as even the oldest villager could remember, this had been the simple rhythm of their lives. And the eldest's recollection, the villagers believed, was the limit of all knowledge.

Neumann persisted, bringing the elders through long meetings in which he described the many advantages. Through Apache he reinterpreted their tradition as one of acceptance and adaptation.

"You do not resist the monsoons," he said. "You

bend to their force. What I bring is the wind of time."

Finally, they yielded, and Neumann had villagers available to work on his projects every day.

Meantime, the Blues continued to slog through a lull as thick as mud. You had to keep moving or it would swallow you up. They didn't even need us to pull security on convoys anymore. Instead, we drew a lot of dirty little details at Quan Loi during the day, and night after night we pulled perimeter guard.

Occasionally, somebody would dream up a recon or something just to get us out of the way. When that happened, Neumann went to Xuan The alone. He loaded his jeep with choice scrounge in the evening and was ready to roll as we saddled up in the morning.

"What you got there?" the LT asked, pointing to a big roll of paper Neumann was carrying.

"Just an idea," he said.

"Don't go overboard," said the LT.

"Time to step up the pace. They're learning."

"Doing what you tell them, you mean," said the LT, "doing what they think you want."

"They learn fast," Neumann said, and climbed into the jeep.

"It's better to stick to things," said the LT. "They understand when you give them things. Bricks and mortar. Plain and simple."

"That's only the beginning," Neumann said, starting the engine. "Step number one."

The rest of us hung around outside our hootches until the sun was up and the lifers had gotten enough coffee in them to realize that the mission they had planned for us wasn't worth the fuel to take us to it. They scrubbed the idea and left us unemployed for another day.

"Another fuckin' nothin'," said Thompson.

"No wickedness for the rested," I said.

"Morgan, you talkin' shit," said Jones.

"Back off, brother," I said.

"Don't be callin' me brother," he said.

"Everybody does," said Tender.

"Not to sound like nigger," said Jones.

"Everybody's Morgan's nigger but the dinks," said Thompson.

"At least the people in Xuan The aren't thieves," I said.

Jones came at me, but I put out my hand.

"I don't mean you," I said. "I'm talking about redneck here. He stole my damned knife."

"You ain't even got a knife," said Jones.

"The motherfucker ripped it off me a long time ago," I said. I do not know why all of a sudden it had become so important to me again. I had been around Thompson for months without bringing it up. But now it nagged at me. The sonofabitch.

"He ain't got any knife either," said Jones, "except that little job he says is for cutting ears."

"He stole my knife, then gave it away," I said. "He's pathological."

"That worse than being a nigger?" said Jones

"I didn't give the motherfucker away," said Thompson. "I sold it to Angelo. He gave it to the LT."

"I guess I had you all wrong, redneck," I said. "I should have known you'd never do anybody a favor for nothing."

162

"You little shit."

The LT broke in before we came to blows.

"Why didn't you tell me about the damned knife?" he asked me.

"I didn't care that you had it," I said. "I didn't want it back. It was the principle of the thing."

"A man starts talking principle," the LT said, "it means he's got an acute case of the ass."

"We all do," said Tender.

"Jones, Thompson, Tender," said the LT, "you meet me in my hootch. I'll find you something to do. Morgan, I want you out in Xuan The today."

"Neumann's already gone with the jeep," I said.

"You can hitch a ride."

"I think I'll just hang around here."

"I want you out of Quan Loi," he said.

"Give me a break," I said.

"That's the idea."


A deuce and a half picked me up at the gate. Its driver was new in country, and very scared. He babbled on about what the others in his unit had told him. How this one hit a mine. How that one drove into an ambush in the rubber plantation just outside the wire.

"They like to hijack whiskey," he said.

"Who does?"

"The VCs," he said. "Use it as medicine. Guess what I'm hauling."

"Whiskey?"

"Wouldn't you just fuckin' know it. I'm glad to have somebody riding shotgun."

"Just for a few miles," I said. "I'm hopping out."

"Alone?"

"Going stalking."

"Holy Jesus" he said. The big truck hit a bump that sent my head banging against the ceiling, my ass bouncing down to the floorboards.

"Nice suspension," I said.

"You been here awhile?"

"Long enough."

"Got any hints about it?"

"Sure. Take a chopper. Ride's smoother. Easier on the ass."

"I mean about making it through alive."

"Stay to the right of the center line," I said. "Don't exceed the posted speed limit. And never, never pass on a curve."

"Hard-core," he said. I pointed to the intersection and he pulled over to the side.

The dirt road was hard and cracked. I slung my rifle and watched the irregular pattern unscroll beneath me as I walked. My throat was as parched as the ground, but I denied myself a drink until I reached the ville. Somewhere toward the middle of your year, you started feeling as if you weren't getting any nearer to the end of it. You had to give yourself some closer goal, even if it was only water at the end of the road.

The wind picked up, carrying dust off the paddies, a hot, dry breeze that didn't even cool my sweat. When I reached a spot where the road cut through a stand of trees, the wind stopped. And so did I, because I heard voices.

I leaped into the shadows and unslung my rifle. The voices went silent. Moving ahead slowly, I tried to see into the trees, but the leaves were a curtain. I saw no one, heard not another word. That did not mean the enemy wasn't there in the jungles. The enemy was everywhere, invisible, watching us.

When I reached the open again I turned around and backed off from the trees like a bandit leaving a bank. By the time it was all right to face forward again, I could see the ville.

Neumann, in the distance, was pacing back and forth, carrying that big roll of paper. Now and then he stopped to consult it, take a measurement and make a few marks.

"Morgan!" he said when he saw me. "I thought they had you out in the bush today."

I didn't answer, just kept trudging toward him.

"It's good to see you," he said. "In fact, it's very good. I've got something I want to try out on you."

"They canceled the recon patrol," I said, and finally treated myself to a few gulps from my canteen. "Thompson and Jones and I got into a pissing contest. The LT sent me here to cool off."

"Good," he said. "Perfect."

Then he took me by the elbow and led me to Tuyet's hootch.

"I don't know why I didn't think of it before," he said when we got inside. "It's such a natural." Then he turned to Tuyet's mother. "How about some of that famous tea, mama-san?"

She looked up quizzically from some rags she was sewing together. Neumann sipped from an imaginary cup, then flipped his eyebrows a couple of times, a comic seducer. Tuyet's mother blushed and bowed and smiled as any mother might.

"Here," he said. "Sit down. Tuyet, come here. I want you to see this, too."

He took the big cylinder from under his arm and unrolled it flat on the floor, weighting it down on one end with a crock and on the other with the case to his flute. It was a large, detailed map of Xuan The: the creek, paddies, treeline, jungle. Every hootch was drawn to scale. The dispensary and the gazebo. Contour lines indicated elevations.

"Mama-san, you get in on this, too," he said. "I may need you to help me with the elders."

She poured tea and sat where Neumann directed her. She craned her neck over the map, then twisted around this way and that, trying to orient herself to what it showed. Tuyet put her hand on Neumann's, and he smiled at her before taking it away to tap on the map.

"Now, what have we got here?" he said.

"What good is a map?" I asked.

"What we have here is an outpost," he said. "A fort in the wilderness."

The mama-san nodded politely whenever he looked at her, and Tuyet edged closer to him on the straw mat.

"Apache says it's been quiet," I said. "They seem to be leaving the ville alone." I did not tell him about the phantom voices in the trees.

"Won't last," he said. "No way. When we have that dispensary up, Xuan The is going to be one attractive target for the NVA. As the rice crop increases—and I'm sure it will—the temptation will be all the stronger."

"Maybe we should just leave things be," I said.

"Too late for that," he said. "Too late. Now,

when you look at the ville, it doesn't look too promising at first from a tactical point of view." He swept his hand across the paper and shook his head. To Tuyet and her mother, the gestures must have seemed as mysterious and ceremonial as a conjurer's. They shook their heads solemnly.

"But it wouldn't take much to turn that around," he said, "not much at all. A little wire, a little digging, some sandbags for a few strong points and most important of all, some light."

"Light?"

"You light up this area here and this one here," he said, poking at the paper, "and there's no way less than a main-force company is going to try to overrun Xuan The. Even the old papa-sans could hold them off. Given proper armament and illumination."

Tuyet's mother finally gave up listening to the words she did not understand and watching gestures whose magic she could not penetrate. She got up from the mat, touched Neumann on the cheek and went to get us more tea.

"It's nonsense to me, Jim," I said.

"All we need is a generator, and I'm already working on that through the pacification people. They're all for it. Not enough new ideas in this war, they say."

"Too many," I said. "None of them good."

"Here, let me show you what I have in mind," he said. "Tuyet, you stay here a minute."

She nodded and lowered her head for a kiss. He touched her hair lightly, distractedly, and then he bounded out of the hootch. I could barely keep up with him in the heat as he marched to the perime-

167

ter and began pointing out where the illumination towers would have to go. His hand stretched upward to the sun, measuring how tall they would have to be to eliminate every dangerous shadow of night.

"Going to have to be steel," he said. "Got to be able to withstand a mortar. Now that might be a little problem, but I'm working on it."

He led me to the dispensary where a small working party was laying bricks. They saw Neumann and waved. Then one of them went through the drill Neumann had taught them. Mortar, brick, level, edge—sharp as a parade. He looked up proudly and, with a silly smile, bowed.

"Number one, papa-san," Neumann said, giving thumbs up. "Number one."

Then to me he said, as if it were a secret, "These people can do anything."

We moved to the edge of the jungle behind the dispensary where Neumann took out a machete and began hacking at the vines.

"This will all have to come out," he said. "It's in too tight to the ville, much too tight. We'll have to clear out a good, wide field of fire and light the sonofabitch up.

"But no sweat," he went on, pulling away a tangle of branches and throwing it clear of the trees. "I been back in all through here, and with one Rome plow I could have this bush busted in less than a day."

"Where is a grunt going to get a Rome plow?" I said.

"I think I've got it figured," he said. "The colonel is hot for this project. And all I have to do is to

168

give him the idea. You think the colonel can't scrounge a plow? The hell he can't. Now come over here. I'll show you the last piece of the defenses."

He took me to the creek, back away from the ville, where he could give me the whole grand panorama.

"You can see it, can't you?" he said. "It's a natural. Three strong points. There, there, there. Why, with lights we won't even need a watchtower. Just some good solid bunkers . . ."

"They can always take out the lights, Jim," I said. "Pop. They're dark."

". . . and the wire will go about like this. Some command-detonated Claymores. And over there by the paddies, that's a weak spot. You can see. The land slopes upward. They'd have a pretty good angle coming in. But I think I've got the ticket."

"A Sheridan tank," I said.

"A moat," he said.

"For Christsake."

"Look," he said. "It would serve two purposes. It would help divert some of the stream water into the paddies. I'm not sure, but we might even be able to fit in another whole rice crop if the irrigation's right. I have to check up on it, but somebody has developed a special new hybrid that might be good. And the moat will have a steep wall on the outside bank and a low, angled incline on the inside. Nobody could come across it against an M-sixty or two in the strongpoint. . . ."

"Jim," I said. But he didn't seem to hear me. He knelt down, scooped up a handful of dusty soil, shook it through his fingers and just kept on talking.

". . . The digging will be easy. The Blues can pitch in. It's no worse than making a fighting hole. They'll go along with it, don't you think? Once they understand what it's for. Maybe we can get a little C-four from the combat engineers and set a charge along here to make it easier."

"Jim . . ."

"Even in the dry season the moat would do the trick. It's not the water as much as the angle of fire. . . ."

He paused and rose slowly from his crouch. He slapped his dusty hands clean against his fatigue pants and then pulled up his hat to wipe the sweat from his face. He closed his eyes for a moment and breathed deeply. Then he was calm.

"It's just that we have to leave them something," he said. "We can't just come here, get all warm inside about how good we are, then walk out on them. They are fine people. Strong. Willing to take direction. They can learn if we help them. . . .

"Morgan," he said, "we have to make a difference here before we abandon them."

"You're pushing too hard," I said.

"You can't move a mountain with your breath," he said.

"Confucius?"

"A venerable Eastern saying I just made up," he said. "The elders, it's the way they think."

"And you will do the thinking for all of them."

"I'm not after power," he said.

"Maybe not," I said, "but, friend, you've got it."

He shrugged and we started back toward the ville. Apache met us halfway.

"They want to talk now," Apache said. "Want map."

"Do they buy the idea?" Neumann asked.

"Worry about guns," Apache said. "Too many guns. But you tell them. They ready."

"Want to join us?" Neumann said.

"I'll stick to the bricks," I said. He accepted that.

It felt good to heft the stones and work the thick mortar with a trowel. The papa-sans watched me to make sure I was doing everything right, and from time to time they corrected the alignment. We stopped at noon for a bit of food and a midday rest. I stretched out under the trees and awakened later to the sound of the flute.

Neumann was out in front in Tuyet's hootch playing slow jazz. Tuyet and her little baby brother sat at his feet. Her mother stood watching him from a distance until he finished. Then she took the little boy by the hand and bowed to Neumann and Tuyet. A white man had come to her once before and then had gone, leaving behind nothing but sorrow and a child. She must have realized that the same thing could happen to Tuyet, but whatever reluctance she might have felt about Neumann, he had overcome it. She led the boy away toward the paddies, only once looking back over her shoulder at her daughter going into the hootch with Neumann.

I got back to work, and eventually Neumann emerged. Tuyet held his hand, a tiny child's grasp. Her mother and baby brother were still in the paddies. She glanced in that direction and paused for a moment trying to find them. Neumann looked and pointed. Tuyet waved, and a small figure far away waved back.

I dried the sweat on the towel around my neck. Tuyet rushed up and helped me. I bowed and she giggled like a schoolgirl.

"Jim friend," she said. "I learn talk good." She was almost as pleased with herself as Neumann was.

"I started the paper work," he said. "She's very happy. I just told her today."

"More supplies?"

"She's coming home with me," he said.

"You'd have to be married."

"There it is," he said, easing her gently to his side.

We loaded the jeep. Neumann kissed Tuyet lightly on the forehead, waved to her mother, and we were off. Apache dozed in the backseat.

"Why the girl?" I asked.

"The last time you were worried about what would happen if I left her."

"I was just asking."

"That's how you do it, Morgan," he said. "You just ask."

"Thi and Donna Jarret, they're different. This is a peasant girl. She doesn't even speak the language."

"She's learning."

"But she's from a different century."

"She's very strong," he said. "She'll do all right."

"Do you think it would be fair to her?"

"It made her happy when I told her."

"She doesn't understand."

"Ah," he said. "But we do, I suppose. We understand everything. And we mustn't let them in

172

on it because they come from a different century. Do you think anything could be worse than what she has already endured? She can make it anywhere. She loves me."

"Love's her ticket out," I said.

When he turned to me, I knew I had finally gone over the line. He was so angry I could barely hear the slow, soft voice of his rage.

"She never asked," he said. "She never hinted that it was what she wanted. I wasn't even sure that she would accept."

"I'm sorry," I said.

"But she has accepted. And I'm happy. And I don't give a damn what you think about that, because all you ever do is think. Think and lean on people. Lean on them until they just can't fucking carry you anymore."

"If there's any way I can help . . ." I said.

"Maybe just by staying away from me," he said. "At least that."


"Don't be a fool, fool," said Jones. "You gonna have to deal with the man."

"This shit's crazy," said Diaz.

"You are where you've been," I said. "I've been here too long."

"Jive," said Jones.

"There it is," said Diaz.

They all blamed me for the distance Neumann had put between us. And I suppose they were right. I had started it. But I had tried to close the distance, too, and Neumann just put me off. After a while I gave up. When Neumann did his jazz out by the bunkers, I stayed back in the stifling hootch. I sat there listening, every night.

"What am I supposed to do?" I said. "We had a difference of opinion."

"Opinion!" said Jones. "Fuck opinion. If the army wanted you to have opinions, it would have issued them."

"Let me tell you something," said Diaz. "This lull ain't gonna last forever. We're gonna have to pay. Someday—CRACK!—out snaps the slack like the smack of a whip. And we gonna have to be together then. All of us."

"You see," said Jones, "we all buh-ruh-thers, brother."

Diaz was right, of course. The lull did not last. And when it ended, I had still not gotten together with Neumann.

The LT called us all to his hootch after dark and said we had a first-light mission. Nobody was going to Xuan The. Apache would explain to them out there what had happened. Be ready to dig in for the night when we get where we're going, he said. Bring rations. Don't count on resupply. It sounded as if we were going to another country.

"What do you think we are?" said Reed. "A bunch of grunts?"

"A man gets used to creature comforts," said Neumann, "it's hard to get him to act like a creature again."

The LT said he figured we'd better get used to it quickly, because this wasn't going to be any cakewalk.

"What kind of dance you talking, then?" said Jones.

"The boogaloo, baby," said the LT. "The big, brass boogaloo."

Neumann continued to avoid me that night. He went off with Jones and some of the others and I went to bed. I did not sleep. Or if I did, I dreamt of being afraid. Somehow even before the LT rousted us in the dark and told us the next morning, I had a premonition what it was going to be. The word haunted me all night: Cambodia.

We were to be the first American unit in, the LT said as we saddled up and checked out our gear in the yellow light of his hootch. We would secure an LZ near the North Vietnamese camp, the enemy command headquarters. First of all, he said, a big C-130 would tip its nose toward the heavens and slide out of its cargo hatch a super-bomb. The bomb would clear an LZ in the jungles and we would follow close behind.

"We're going after the damned dink Pentagon," said Jones, more in awe than anything else.

"That's the idea," said the LT, then he told us to mount up and move out to the chopper pad.

The pilots and crews hadn't gotten there yet. Quan Loi was very still. Reed looked at the LT's map of the zone we'd be operating in and was surprised, and a little disappointed, to find that except for the names it didn't seem much different from Vietnam. I slung down my rucksack, leaned up against the cold brown side of the Huey and lighted a cigarette. The smoke hung in the air like fog. Thompson paced back and forth, his face tormented by tics. I felt a hand on my shoulder.

"Back to normal," Neumann said. "You have another one of those?"

I dug the plastic case out of the deep breast pocket of my fatigues and gave it to him. He saw my hand shaking.

"Not a bad day for an invasion," he said.

"If you've got to have one."

The crews arrived and started cranking up the choppers. I picked up my gear and dragged it out of the wind to where Neumann had piled his. Tender was nearby, mumbling into his handset. Diaz stayed close to Bones, head bent to chest, hands folded. Bones watched him, and when Diaz looked up, Bones nodded. This time the prayers were not even hidden. This time we were going to die.

"Shake it off," said Neumann.

"Bad," I said. "Very bad."

"Been worse," he said.

"I'm not so sure."

Neumann sniffed, stubbed and stripped his cigarette and said, "Look at them. You going to let them go in there without you?"

"It's not right," I said.

"What is?" he said.

The light seemed to be coming up when the LT passed the order to move out. It was dawn, the first one, the false one, when we mounted the choppers.

I only knew we crossed the border because the pilot turned and smiled and gave us thumbs up. You'd think the invasion of a sovereign nation would amount to something a little more than a thumb jerking in the air and a stupid smile. Down below, the real dawn was just beginning. Fires still burned in the distance where the B-52s had hit during the night. We flew high over the unfamiliar land until the copilot spotted the LZ, a huge crater in what looked like a rubber plantation. The trees had all fallen outward from the center of the blast and looked like the spokes of a wheel.

We banked to the right, dropped down and began to fly contour. The top branches of the trees scraped the chopper's skids and slapped up against the bottom as the pilot hugged the curves of the terrain. I watched the ground carefully, but I saw nothing through the trees. No Pentagon. No wire. Not even a bunker.

When we reached the crater, the pilot pulled up fast, raising the chopper's nose high into the air to get the rotors to act as a brake. Then we hovered and I leaped into the incoming fire.

The choppers got out safely as the fire continued to stammer. I felt it coming in my direction, groping around me, seeking me out as I lay on my stomach beside the stump of a tree. The incoming fire was nervous but not heavy. It sounded like AKs from no more than three positions around the crater. I looked behind me. Diaz was up on one knee behind a higher stump to my right.

I raised my head a little, then I heard the whip crack and felt a sickening wind brush across my face. I was familiar with the sound. It was the crack of bullets coming close. Though it was the first time I felt the wind, I knew what it was, too. Then Diaz screamed. The round that had tickled my lips had crashed into his flesh.

His equipment clattered as he fell. He writhed on the ground with his hands on his groin. Blood pulsed between his fingers.

"They got my dick" he cried. "God help me, mother of Mary, they got my dick."

He rolled to one side and then to the other. He brought up one blood-soaked hand, tried to make the sign of the cross, but stopped midway and grabbed for the wound again. Bones crawled up as I laid down a long cover of fire. The rifle shook madly in my hands. I let it aim itself. I had no target.

When I looked back, the medic was working on Diaz, who arched upward like a wrestler trying to break a pin hold.

All the fire was ours now. Neumann came up beside me. He leaned over Diaz and touched his soft, crying face. The bottom of Neumann's bandoleer just barely grazed the wound.

They took Diaz out on the first available Huey slick. Bones said Diaz's penis was intact and that he would probably be using it before we used ours because the slug had struck a bone. That meant Medevac back to the World. A pretty good wound, we all agreed.

It was all ass-backward. The fights you feared were the easiest, and the ones that seemed so easy went bad.

Cambodia turned out to be nothing much at all. We took a few casualties, but the only guy who was killed was a replacement. We didn't even know his name. I had been scared of finding the NVA Pentagon, but it wasn't there. I'd been scared of the Chinese coming into it, as they had in Korea, but not a peep. It was just the same old shit in new surroundings.

It got so that some of the Blues actually liked it in the plantations and old colonial towns of Cambodia. There wasn't much barbed wire or junk lying around. The roads were good. There were flowers all over the place and nicely built hootches up on stilts. But we could see what was happening as we moved through Cambodia day after day. It wasn't going to stay beautiful. The war was going to be there for a good long time.

On the last day of the operation they put us into the square of what had been a little plantation town called Snoul. A light observation helicopter had set down in the middle of the square with engine trouble. We were supposed to secure the place until a big Chinook helicopter could come in and lift it out.

Nothing much remained of Snoul. The shells of bombed-out buildings bordering the square showed traces of what the town had been: a quiet French colonial place in pastel yellow stucco and red tile roofs. I had heard what had happened. An armor column from the 11th Armored Cavalry Regiment met its first real resistance there on the drive up the Fishhook weeks before. The tanks had taken incoming when a reconnaissance unit entered the town. The unit pulled back, then the column returned in force, laying down tremendous fire. Then came the jets. They blasted Snoul to rubble.

A line of fresh graves marked the far end of the square. They were the civilian dead. If the North Vietnamese had lost any men, they had carried off the bodies so that when the tanks returned the next morning—their crews tense for another fight— the GIs found only the bodies of women and children. Suddenly, victory sucked. And when there was no fight, the relieved and guilty tank crews went out of control, looting the town for liquor and trinkets.

When we landed, the place was deserted except for the two LOH pilots out in full view, stripped to the waist, tinkering with the motor like teenagers fixing the car on a hot summer afternoon. We set up a ragged perimeter and waited.

Neumann began poking around the ruins, but I did not want to see any more than I had to. I had not wanted to go into Cambodia in the first place. And now I wanted out.

Maybe we should have learned something there about what war does to dreams and other pretty things. But we did not. It just felt eerie, that's all. Millions of flowers blossoming bright as fire in carefully landscaped beds next to burnt-out buildings. It was the wrong spot for a war.

"Come over here," Neumann shouted. "I want to show you something."

He waited for me, a distance away from the flattened square, outside a remote row of frame houses that remained untouched. When I got there, he motioned me past the beautiful flame trees on either side of the door. As my eyes got used to the dark, I saw that the walls were covered with yellowing newspaper photographs of North Vietnamese soldiers. A Chinese-made SKS rifle leaned up against the back wall, and beside it lay an ammunition belt.

We decided to leave them where they were as a kind of testimony to what had happened and why.

We placed a few M-16 bullets next to the rifle, just to record our presence.

"Looks like an officer's quarters," said Neumann as he looked through the drawers of a little bureau in the corner. "They've been here quite awhile."

"Must've had to get out in a big hurry to leave all this stuff," I said.

"Or else they intended to be back."

After the invasion I tried to make peace with Xuan The. I did not go there right away because the action picked up a bit and I had to stay with the unit. But I did show an interest. The interruption while we were in Cambodia seemed to have taken some of the momentum out of the project. Neumann would not admit that anything was wrong, so I pressed Apache for information.

"Numba one GI," he said of Neumann. "You numba one, too."

"You're easy to please," I said.

"Oh, no," he said. "Very hard. I please everybody."

"What about VC?"

"Numba ten," he said.

"I mean do they come to the ville at night? Do they collect taxes?"

"VC stay away."

"Why?"

"VC not like American GI," he said.

"You mean they've conceded Xuan The?"

He looked at me puzzled.

"Have they given up on the ville?" I said.

"VC never give," he said. "VC take."

"Then why are they leaving Xuan The alone?"

"Because," he said, "the people tell me so."

The Blues weren't much more help than Apache. With the exception of Tender and Jones, they weren't going out on Good Dink Duty anymore. Tender went because of Tuyet. Jones for the jazz.

"You ought to make it sometime," he told the new brother we called Barracuda until that got too cumbersome and we shortened it to Cuda. "He'd play for you if you went. Good sounds. Very blue. Sometimes when the rains come, all the dinks gather under this little bandshell thing they have there in the square and the man plays for them. You'd dig it. They do."

"No shit?" said Cuda.

"Dink soul," said Jones. "They dig our sounds."

"Dig our menthol cigarettes, too," said Bones. "Dig Wrigley gum. Dig Crest."

"Is the dispensary finished?" I asked.

"He's having trouble scrounging," said Reed. "Supplies dried up. You'd think they got our caches instead of us getting theirs."

"Nothin' to do out there," Angelo complained. "Repair this. Repair that. Fix the dike. Might as well be painting rocks in the colonel's garden."

"LT says he has some angles working," said Reed.

"Somebody's bucking him out there," said Jones.

"I heard the dink province chief got a case of the ass about it," said Reed.

"How come?"

"Ville don't need him. Just needs Neumann. Chief would rather blow it away than build it up," said Reed.

"Something to that point of view," said Thompson.

"If the LT can't scrounge what he needs, then it just can't be scrounged, that's all," said Jones.

"I'd still go back, I think, if they got some brick," said Reed.

"I'd give it a go," said Cuda.

"No sweat," said Angelo.

"Got to give the man credit," said Reed.

Next morning they had us saddle up for cache-hunting. We climbed on the choppers and took off before somebody discovered that the ARVN were already there.

"They dinks, ain't they?" said Thompson. "Let's tussle 'em."

The LT said no, and we headed back to Quan Loi again. It was another empty day, another chance to hitch to Xuan The. But this time it was my idea.

A blue haze slept on the ville, on the hootches, the paddies, smoothing them against the horizon. The air was absolutely still, and the smoke from their fires went up in straight, high columns. The flowers were beginning to bloom, flashes of red and yellow in the fog. And the rice was just poking up out of the water, a bright, new green.

But something was wrong. Nobody was in the paddies. There were no children in sight. Once I got to the ville I saw the people huddled inside their hootches as if against the rain. They watched me warily as I passed, and when I waved to a little boy, his mother drew him back farther into the

184

hootch out of sight. When I reached Tuyet's hootch, Apache was there talking excitedly to her mother, who just shook her head and wept.

"Numba ten," he said when he saw me.

"Where's Neumann? Tuyet?"

"Tuyet go," said Apache, pointing out the door toward the jungles. "Neumann chase her."

"Gone where?"

"Tell nobody," he said. "Neumann come. They have tea. Like always. He angry. Go to creek bank to sit. She go away."

"Why is everyone so scared?"

"Neumann shout. Think somebody know where Tuyet run."

"Which way did Neumann go?"

He pointed toward an opening in the trees, the beginning of a trail. I took my rifle off my shoulder and checked the clip. Tuyet's mother screamed. I put the rifle down and went to calm her. She cowered away from me.

"Tell her I am going to bring them back," I said.

The jungle dripped with the night's rain. I didn't have a machete, so I had to use the trails. It was still slow, hard work. The paths were overgrown. Leaves and vines ripped my hands. Mosquitoes bit through my fatigues. I put my hand on the trunk of a tree to steady myself and ended up scalded by a swarm of fire ants.

The farther I went, the darker it got, dusky and closed in. The trees ahead bent with the curve of human spines. The limbs stretched out like ghostly arms, beckoning me on. The jungle was alive with the risk of others.

I heard sounds and followed them, but they

turned out to be vines slapping one another or the skittering flight of small animals. Then, finally, I saw something on the ground. It was a piece of checkered cloth, the kind Tuyet sometimes wore on her head. I looked for signs that someone else had been with her at the spot, but the floor of the jungle did not offer any more clues. I pushed on deeper, and for some reason it wasn't until I saw them that I even considered she might be with anyone but Neumann.

The two of them, Tuyet and a young man, were standing at the edge of a small clearing. But the moment I raised my rifle, he vanished. I could not get him in my sights. Tuyet stood motionless. I thought the man may have been back a pace in the jungle, covering her. I stayed hidden where I was.

Then she turned around and started toward me, walking slowly across the clearing, not frightened at all. I flicked the safety back on, cracked a vine to warn her somebody was near, then called her name.

She looked up, then she glanced back over her shoulder to where she had been. I came out of my hiding place.

"Tuyet, are you all right?"

She took one last, quick look behind her and ran to me.

"Who was there, Tuyet?"

She pretended she did not understand.

"Why did you come here?" I said. She looked at the bandana in my hand. I gave it to her, and she pulled it slowly through her fingers to straighten it.

"Why?" I said.

She took my hand and led me to where I thought I had seen the man. She knelt and urged me down next to her, then lifted a vine and pulled back a curtain of leaves. A few awkward, fluffy bird chicks tried to hide. Several eggs remained unhatched. And on the floor of the nest lay a handful of grain. Tuyet reached into her waistband, pulled out a small, knotted olive-drab handkerchief and opened it. Inside was more grain. She took a few kernels and sprinkled them into the nest.

I stood and she looked up at me, sweet and troubled.

"Let's go back, Tuyet," I said.

"Baby-san," she said, gently lowering the branches back over the nest. "Hungry."

"I saw a man," I said, and this time she didn't pretend not to understand me.

"No man," she said. "Only feed baby-san."

The foolish thing was, I believed her. Or did not believe in myself. Or wanted to trust her. Or wanted at least to be able to trust. All of those things.

"Jim is worried about you," I said. "We'd better go back."

I followed her out of the jungle. She knew the way. In fact, the ville was really only a few hundred meters from where we had stood. I must have gotten myself lost in the maze of trails when I was going in.

"What are you doing here?" Neumann demanded when we came out of the bush.

"Another bum mission," I said. "I came out to work."

"It was stupid to go into the jungle alone," he said.

"I found her, didn't I?"

He turned away from me and started toward the jeep.

"I'll take you back," he said.

"I'd rather stay and help."

"There's nothing to do today," he said. Then he stopped and stood a moment. "Look, I scared her. That's all. I was angry. Not at her. Just angry. Restless. Bad day. Fucked-up weather. Everything stalled. I was afraid I might have hurt her with my yelling. That's why I went after her. She knows the jungle better than I do. She can take care of herself. I just wanted to set things straight."

"Does she sneak off a lot? I saw a man."

"She does what she wants," he said.

"I'll hitch a ride back if you want me to."

"Maybe that would be better this time."

Then he turned and left me standing there. When he got to Tuyet's hootch, she was standing in the doorway. She took his hand, held it up to her face and glanced curiously in my direction before they finally went inside.


Contact with the enemy continued to increase, but it was still nothing like what we expected at this time of the year. Even on the slow days, the Blues did not generally volunteer to go with Neumann.

When he came to me and asked me to spend another day with him in the ville, I was glad to go. I thought maybe I could encourage him this time, make amends. He seemed to need help from

188

somebody. He didn't blow jazz anymore. He didn't even smoke with us at night. From time to time he would come to the hootch late, dizzy with too much whiskey.

I got the LT's permission, and we left Quan Loi early in the morning in Neumann's jeep. He was quiet, nursing a bad head.

A spectacular red dawn grew over the greening paddies, and thunderheads rolled in from the east behind the sun. The road was muddy but still firm. Clouds shadowed Xuan The, and a haze came off the paddies veiling everything. A light breeze blew in from the creek bringing with it the smell of stagnation.

No one waited for us at the edge of town that morning. The ville seemed deserted except for the plumes of smoke rising from a few of the hootches. Even the sound of our engine didn't attract a crowd. We pulled up near the dispensary and waited until Tuyet came.

She smiled, kissed Neumann lightly. Then she bowed to me.

"Work today?" she asked.

"No brick. No tin. Maybe tomorrow," said Neumann.

The haze was burning thin, and the villagers were coming out of their hootches to go to the paddies. A few approached us expectantly.

"Not yet," he said. "Not today."

They shuffled away.

We stood near the dispensary. Its walls had risen no higher than the level of Neumann's eyes. The last half-meter was made with chunks of stone and brick he had earlier marked as unsalvageable.

Two scrawny dogs nosed around inside the structure, but not eagerly.

"It's slowing down," Neumann said.

"Looks to me as if it has stopped," I said.

"I don't mean just the building. The people are getting anxious. I'm losing them."

"I don't suppose they care much about red tape."

"The elders know I am trying," he said. "But I'm afraid about the inertia."

An old woman wandered around in the square. She moved slowly and aimlessly, bracing on a thick walking stick. Her face was sunken and her clothes ragged. Neumann didn't pay any attention to her. She moved a little closer.

"Trouble is, there's not much I can do for them," Neumann said. "I don't want to get them used to charity. I want them to work. I don't want to be an outsider."

Neumann scraped with his fingernail some dried mortar bulging from chinks in the wall. The old lady moved up toward us. I looked at her and smiled. She stared back with an odd expression in her yellowed eyes. Her face was the color of dead leaves. Her hands trembled. When she got up close, she began to wail.

I reached out to touch her and she struck. The blow was light, just a tap. Then she struck again and again with her stick, screaming words I did not understand. I moved back away from her. Neumann held her arms at her sides as the men ran to us. She glared at Neumann as the men led her off.

"She's a little crazy," said Neumann. "Don't let her worry you. She came from the North. Her

190

family is all dead. Too much war. The village takes care of her."

The elders invited us into a hootch and made an elaborate apology. They asked one of the younger men to show me the rice fields under full cultivation. Neumann came along. We got the guided tour, like visiting dignitaries.

Afterward, Neumann and I worked alone in the unfinished dispensary. We used hoes and rakes to smooth and level the earth floor.

"I want to put in brick floors someday," he said. "But the walls and roof come first."

It was easy labor and both of us took it slowly. There was no use in finishing it.

Later, Tuyet brought some lunch and sat down to eat with us. She had some kind of fish stew for herself and beans and bacon for us. I watched her and made a big deal out of how good it was to be in Xuan The again. She tried to smile. Neumann seemed to be going out of his way to avoid meeting her eyes. After we had finished, she took the empty tins.

"Thank you," I said. *"Cam on."*

"Need more Cs," she said, and I could not figure out why she was telling it to me.

"I'll see what I can do," I said.

"They've been at them again, haven't they?" said Neumann.

"No eat Cs," she said. "Just you. Just Blues."

"I brought a couple of cases out a short time ago, Tuyet," he said.

"All gone, Jim," she said.

"They've been eating the rations, and I told you they shouldn't."

"No, Jim."

"Don't you understand?" he said. "They must not get used to this food. Someday it will be gone."

She turned and left us sitting in the shade of one of the walls.

"I shouldn't punish her like that," he said after a time.

"She probably understands," I said. "It will be better when the work gets started again."

"It's hard to know when she understands and when she doesn't," he said. "She has suffered a lot of lies. They all have. They're not fools. They have learned to distrust."

"I'm sure they believe your intentions," I said. "The LT will come through. It's only a matter of time."

"I may have more time here than you think," he said. "The papers for getting married are all bogged down. The government apparently doesn't like to lose women young enough to breed."

"Does Tuyet know?"

"I told her about it."

"Disappointed?"

"It didn't show," he said. "She said she believed me. And I meant it. I will extend as long as it takes."

"Is that what she wants?"

"I love her," he insisted. "It's as easy as that. I love her."

It was raining when the LT mustered us out of our bunks in the dark. The drops rattled on the roof and splashed in the puddles outside the door. They came straight down like a curtain of beads.

Neumann and I got up and helped rouse the others. Then, as they were getting ready, we dashed through the downpour to the LT's hootch.

"Chopper down," the LT said. "Ground fire got it on the way to a first-light recon. Pilots report negative contact after going down. But they say it's as dark as a motherfucker out there, and they don't sound happy."

A few of the Blues were drifting in, shaking off the water, then sitting down or leaning against the walls.

"Neumann," said the LT, "you might as well join us on this one. The chopper dropped just outside Xuan The."

"Shit, man," said Cuda. "Why not just let the

man tool on out there by his own self? Just like always."

"We'll move out in ten minutes," said the LT.

"It's his damned ville," whined Cuda.

"Muffle it," said Jones.

"Just a damned sniper," said Cuda. But that was the last of it. Jones had moved up next to him and loomed there as accommodating as granite.

Of course, we all knew that in this case Cuda was right. It was just going to be another one of those wet, miserable false alarms. Sure there were NVA prowling the jungles around Xuan The, but they kept their distance, especially when daylight was coming.

The choppers had already started to crank by the time we got to the chopper pad, so we piled into them on the run. The rain had petered out to a drizzle for the time being. Within a few minutes we came up over the road to Xuan The. Then we circled to the right so we could approach the landing zone from opposite the trees where the shots had been fired. As we made our approach, the crew on the ground set a flare on a paddy dike to mark their position. Our choppers hovered just above the water, sending up a wall of spray and churning the rice shoots in great, circular waves.

I jumped out into the turbulent waters, disoriented by the white, stroboscopic light of the flare. My footing slipped. I fell backward. My hand sank into the mud and excrement at the bottom of the paddy, but I managed to keep my rifle dry above my head. I struggled up and moved toward the stricken chopper. By the time I reached it, our helicopters had peeled off, and the only sound was their receding chatter and the laughing obscenities of the other Blues floundering around in the muck.

"Been any shooting?" the LT asked the pilot.

"Not yet," he said. "Looked pretty bad at first. Couldn't see a *damned* thing."

The overcast sky was beginning to go pink over Xuan The. The pilot had put down about three hundred meters from the westernmost edge of the ville's triangle and about twenty-five meters south of the creek near a rickety latrine perched over the water.

"Where did the shots come from?" asked the LT.

We had circled up into a sloppy perimeter following the dikes. From a distance it did not look as if anything was moving in Xuan The. No lights, not even a cooking fire. Beyond the latrine I could just barely make out the shadow of the treeline behind the dispensary.

"It was only one burst, I think," said the pilot. "My crew chief here said he picked up tracers from the jungle over there. He returned fire as we were coming down. Don't see what he could have hit. Too dark."

"Any movement since?"

"Nothing."

"Maybe we'd better get a squad down into the ville," said the LT.

"What's wrong with Morgan and me?" Neumann said. "I mean, why frighten them?"

"We could put three, maybe four blooker rounds into the middle of the square," said Thompson. "Just to call reveille."

"They're more likely to talk if just the two of us go in," said Neumann.

"Want 'em to talk?" said Thompson. "I'll show you how to get them to talk."

"Shove it, Thompson," said the LT.

"That's sort of what I had in mind, sir," said Thompson. And laughing, he waded back into the paddies to share his joke with the others.

"You mind, Morgan?" asked the LT.

"No," I said. "Hell no." After all, the sky was brightening up. Xuan The was ours in the light.

"I'll follow the dikes," said Neumann. "You swing around and come up the creek bed, just in case."

It was just like the backyard war games I played as a kid, drawing maps with a stick in the dust: Here's the big tree with the fort in it, there's the Naughtons' garage, you go around there and I'll sneak up on them like this, and when I whistle like a bird, you attack. What kind of bird? A yellow-bellied sapsucker, stupid, now move out.

I slogged my way to a dike and followed it to the creek. Before going down the bank, I glanced back over the paddies. Neumann had gotten to within two hundred meters of the ville. He made some effort to be inconspicuous, doing a kind of duck walk behind a berm. But his head bobbed up above the cover like a target in a shooting gallery. It didn't matter. I could see the LT, back at the chopper, laughing it up, and the Blues playing grab-ass.

The creek bank was steep and slippery. I made about fifty meters on its muddy edge, but it went so slowly, what with sliding downhill all the time and maneuvering to get back up again, that I finally just waded in waist-deep and bucked the current of the stream.

The smell got putrid as I approached the latrine. It didn't come from the water itself so much as from years of shit caked on the superstructure. I moved up to my nipples in the water to make a wide arc around the stench. By the time I got to within seventy-five meters of the first hootch, my legs were getting weak under me. The mud and current made the trip much harder than it looked.

A rifle cracked. Just one shot. It sounded like an M-16, and it came from the direction of the ville.

I did not raise my head above the bank. If Neumann had fired, it was because he had found a target. And that meant trouble. I moved faster now, closer to the high bank.

Two more shots. A burst. Another burst. Silence.

I scrambled up the bank and flattened out just before the top. Then I darted to the nearest hootch.

The ville lay silent. Tuyet's hootch was the sixth in line in front of me. I wanted to get there because I was worried about them, and I knew that was where Neumann would go, too. I crouched. When I peeked around the corner, I could see nothing moving. No life at all. I ran for the next hootch and waited for the bullets to find me. Silence. I darted from cover to cover, and the scuffling sound of my feet was all I heard.

When I got to the hootch just before Tuyet's, I thought I saw a shadow moving near the dispensary. Then I heard somebody coughing and gagging. I broke for Tuyet's door.

I could just barely make out Neumann's big shape inside. The room was choked by gunsmoke.

My eyes slowly got used to the darkness. Neumann struggled to get a new clip into his M-16, but his hands fumbled out of control. A smear of vomit showed on his chin.

The back of the hootch was vague with smoke and shadows, but I could see enough. A man in a tattered old tan shirt and black peasant's pants lay on his side. His face looked young, what was left of it. A bullet had hit him just above the nose. Tuyet sprawled grotesquely with her head on the young man's hip. Blood poured from a single hole in her left breast. The bodies of her baby brother and mother lay contorted in the opposite corner. Their limbs were tangled together. Blood spotted and ran in little rivulets in the dirt.

"Neumann!"

He whirled toward me.

"I killed them," he said. Then he chambered a round, the rifle pointed toward my belly. I dropped my weapon. The low sun struck the barrel of his rifle and made a shining halo of its muzzle. His head shook. It was as if he were denying what I could see with my eyes.

"Going to kill me, too?" I said.

He lowered the rifle slowly. He looked as if he were about to speak when the first bullet spun him to the ground.

The rest missed both of us. I hit the dirt as the bullets ripped away pieces of the doorframe and stitched across the thatching of the wall.

"You hit?"

"Thigh," he said. He crawled out of the light in the doorway and ripped open his fatigue pants. He seemed to have come out of the daze. But even the danger did not release me from what I had seen. My eyes darted among the open, empty courtyard, Neumann's wound and the dead.

"I'm OK," he said, tying a dressing around his leg. There was quite a bit of blood on his clothes, but it seemed to be a clean wound.

The machine-gun fire came from the treeline. We stayed on our bellies as the shots snapped overhead. About ten meters from the doorway lay the only cover, a pile of rocks and debris left over from the dispensary. The only protection the hootch offered was shadow. The walls wouldn't stop anything. Shadows were small comfort. Neumann moved first.

He took off fast despite the wound, and crashed down behind the mound before the machine-gunner had a chance to fire. Then Neumann fired a short burst, and I took the cue. I broke for the mound as he emptied his clip into the trees.

The mound was better than nothing, but not much better. Our ass was uncovered, and if the NVA had a few men to spare, I knew they would be sending them down the creek to get behind us and cut us off. I could not come up with any good ideas. There was nothing but flat, clear ground between us and the dispensary. It was a good thirty meters away, and the machine-gunner seemed to have a clear field of fire for the whole distance.

I looked at Neumann full of questions, only some of which had to do with survival. His eyes had gone glassy. The apex of fear and fatigue, courage and despair, all look the same in a man's eyes. I guessed despair. I guessed wrong.

Neumann suddenly shifted to his good side. He

leaped to his feet and ran the long run. I fired off a burst of twenty, the whole clip. It must have done some good. The enemy bullets pounded behind Neumann, but he beat them to cover.

I reloaded and kept firing as Neumann disappeared behind the dispensary. When he was gone, time slowed. The machine gun alternated between me and the dense woods where Neumann had gone. I fired absently. I couldn't see so much as a muzzle flash, so I could only fire in the right general direction. I imagined the enemy soldiers laughing as my shots tattered the trees high above their heads or harassed the vegetation on their flanks.

Something scuffed behind me. I rolled to my back with my rifle aimed straight down my body. My eyes beat my finger. I held fire. It was the LT, and he was crawling up fast.

"We're out on your flanks," he said, catching his breath. "Where's Neumann?"

"Out after the machine-gunner," I said.

"What happened?"

I fired another burst into the forest.

"He killed Tuyet and her family," I said. "In there." I pointed with my rifle to the hootch.

The LT waited until the machine gun pivoted away from us, then he crawled to the doorway. He looked inside and came back quickly.

"Fuckin' trouble," he said.

An M-16 burst in the jungle. An explosion.

Then Neumann came upright and limping out of the treeline, his torn pants leg black with blood.

"Get your ass down!" the LT screamed. But

Neumann kept right on walking, dragging his rifle by the barrel through the mud.

Another machine gun opened up from somewhere off to the right of the first. Neumann was out of its sight, concealed from the gun by two hootches. He kept walking in a daze as the bullets scored our position. This new gun had a better angle on us than the one Neumann put out of commission. The LT and I pulled back as far as we could along the berm.

Neumann finally went to his belly and crawled painfully, pushing off with his good leg. When he reached us, the LT pulled him over the mound and held him down.

The ground shook. Someone had called in our artillery, but it was sauntering around too far to the left. We all heard the thunk of their mortar before the hootch behind us exploded and the debris clattered down around us.

"Fuckin' mortar," the LT said. Neumann started to get up to his knees. But the LT dove on him and brought him flat as another hootch disintegrated to our right.

"All right, hero," said the LT, holding him. The thatch and bamboo was burning on both our flanks now. I heard somebody crying.

The LT let go of Neumann and fired a long, sweeping burst low into the trees. The air split with a piercing cry that meant the LT had hit his mark.

"The motherfucker," the LT said.

The next mortar shell landed directly on Tuyet's hootch. I watched the first fragments tear off the

LT's face. I watched him bleed for an instant before I felt my own wound.

The shrapnel was just a hot wind at first, rustling my clothes as it hit. But once inside, it seemed to ignite. My back and ass seared with fire. I screamed. Then the machine gun stitched a pattern close to our position, and I forgot about the pain.

I returned fire and suddenly realized that I was firing alone. One M-16 against everything they had. Neumann wasn't shooting. Finally, I called out to him. But when I turned to look, I saw the blood spotting the front of his fatigue shirt. His arm was crooked unnaturally behind his back. His eyes gazed straight at me, but they weren't asking for help.

Our artillery started pummeling the treeline. And once it got accurate, the machine gun stopped. All Neumann could do was to breathe and to bleed. My pain had gone to numbness. I did not know how badly I was hit. My hand came away red from the wound.

I crawled to Neumann, raised him up a little and wrenched his arm from behind his neck. He took a pained breath and closed his eyes.

"They're coming up now," I told him. "They'll have a chopper in soon."

I looked across Lieutenant Selder's contorted body, across the flat dirt yard now littered with the remains of the hootches, across the bright mirror of the paddies rippling in the heat. Bones and four other Blues moved cautiously toward us.

"Medic!" I yelled. It might not have been much more than a whisper, coming out. "Medic!"

Then a plume of water flew up in front of Bones. When the water column fell, nobody was left standing.

Our artillery answered their mortar, but the dinks got off a few more rounds. The first shell hit the dispensary. Neumann watched the explosion cut a chunk out of the top of one wall. The rest of the brick and block held.

Next the mortar bracketed our position with two shots. I knew the third would be on target. I rolled close to Neumann and pulled the LT's body on top of us. The round landed just to our right, and the LT's corpse took the brunt of it. It flailed with the concussion, the biting shrapnel. His blood poured onto my face.

When the mortar was silent for a few minutes, I rolled him back off us and wiped my face on my shirt sleeve. The LT's body was nothing but scraps. It had saved our lives.

Our artillery was walking back and forth like a giant in the treeline now. In the thunder of the shells, the mortar was silenced. I lay there, the pain returning, and waited.

"Who's hurt?"

It was Jones. He darted toward us from the creek bed.

"LT's dead. Neumann hit bad. Bones and some others in the paddy," I said. Tender came up behind Jones with the radio. He called in the Dustoff.

"You're hit, too," said Jones.

"How bad?" I said.

"Move your ass," he said. "Wiggle it." I did.

"Still works," he said.

The artillery had by then walked a long way

back into the jungle and the explosions were far enough away from us that they sounded like muffled drumming.

The chopper arrived quickly. It landed twenty-five meters away, kicking up a cloud of debris. The medics ran toward us. Jones sent one with a litter to the paddy for Bones and the others. Then he helped lift Neumann onto another litter. Before moving him to the chopper, the medic looked Neumann over, tore away some of his clothes and dusted the worst wounds. Then he administered the morphine.

All the while Neumann stared straight at me. I was the only other witness left. There was denial in his face. Denial and defeat. Then the medics carried him away.

Another medic dusted my ass and said I'd survive. Bones and the others had taken bad hits when the mortar round landed near them. I decided I could wait until the wounded Blues and villagers had all been evacuated. I wanted to fly out with the LT and the rest of the dead.

"We got us a few back there," said Jones. "You well enough to see?"

He helped me up and supported me as I limped to the edge of the creek. Four NVA soldiers sprawled on the bank, their blood draining down the muddy slope, turning the dirty water a sickening shade of red. Thompson rifled their pockets. He modestly claimed only two as his own. But he wanted the names of all four.

"Can't tell which was which," he said. "All look the same when you're wastin' 'em."

I moved back into the shattered square. The

204

rubble of Tuyet's hootch disclosed nothing now. It was all over. Eventually, they buried all the stark, physical evidence of what had happened that morning in Tuyet's family grave, all but the fragments it left in Neumann and me.

The official inquiry, of course, was a joke. Not that we were laughing about it going in. At first it looked like real trouble. We did not understand what the army had in mind. We thought it might really want to get to the bottom of what had happened in Xuan The, what the hell had gone wrong. At least, we figured, it would be looking for somebody to take the fall. We were worried about how it would turn out, but at least we thought there would have to be some kind of conclusion about what Neumann had done.

As it turned out, the only thing the army lawyers were concerned about was to make sure nobody knew anything that would make a stink later on. They didn't want any of us going back home with something stuck to the bottom of his boots. Who's got shit on his shoes? That's all the army lawyers wanted to find out.

And, of course, our problem was what we didn't know. I didn't know then who the man in the NVA shirt really was. Nobody knew whether the man in the hootch had a rifle. I had not seen one, but I hadn't exactly had a chance to make an inspection. When the investigators went out looking, they didn't find any weapons in the wreckage, but that didn't prove anything either. In Vietnam if something had any value, it was gone the moment you took your eyes off it. We didn't know why

Neumann had fired or what he had seen. When you got right down to it, we didn't know shit.

And the colonel running the inquiry did not even know as much as we did. He did not know what Xuan The had meant to us or how we had come to feel about Tuyet and her family. He did not know Neumann. And so it was easy for him to conclude that there was no evidence of failure, no problem at all. We had gone to Xuan The that day under combat conditions. The place had turned out to be swarming with NVA. It was, after all, a war. And there had been a stranger, probably VC, in the hootch when Neumann walked in. For the colonel that was reason enough to explain why Neumann had fired.

It was only when the inquiry was over and Neumann was freed, after we had shared our testimony and tried to put it all together, that we began to understand about the law, how it deals only with what is put before it and does not concern itself with what it does not know. But we were still not satisfied. It wasn't nearly enough for the colonel to say there was no problem with what had happened in Xuan The. Not guilty is not the same thing as innocent.

# 5
# Fragments

Fragments. Pieces of metal. Bent, misshapen. Pieces of time. A moment here, a moment there. You took hits, but you kept moving, you just kept moving toward home. You flew all night, all day. Continent to continent. Century to century. And time spun beneath you like the turning earth.

You tried in vain to make connections. You yearned for explanations, exculpations. You remembered the details, the moments of horror. But you remembered the closeness, too, your pure mortal reliance on others. And no matter how you put the fragments together, they did not make a whole.

You wanted to be home again, home where old connections were waiting like strong, open bonds ready to embrace you and hold you firm. You wanted to plug yourself into them again: parents, friends, ideas and images as innocent as youth. And there were times on the way home when the whole country seemed to beckon to you like a sweet mother offering comfort.

But there were other times when you realized you were Lazarus back from the dead, and you needed to report what you had seen. You needed to answer all their questions because maybe that would give you the distance you needed to make the thing whole again. And, yes, you wanted them to understand because they were your jury; they had sent you off to war, and now that you had returned, they alone had the power to honor and excuse.

Then there was Neumann. The Blues all expected that I would be going to see him right away. On my last day in Quan Loi, they gave me messages for him. Thompson said to tell him he should have gotten a medal for what he had done. The others did not even look at him when he said it, and he just walked away. Jones told me to tell Neumann that he missed the music. Cuda did not know Neumann that well, but he knew the legend, and he wanted me to give Jim his best. They made me promise to write back about how he was doing. They were all concerned about his wounds. But there was something else, something nobody had spoken about since the inquiry. And it was finally Tender who said it.

"Find out about Xuan The," he said.

"It's over," said Jones, and he began to pace back and forth in the dust by the bunkers. "It just happened."

"I bet that dude in the hootch fired on him," said Cuda.

"They didn't find a weapon," said Tender. "Morgan didn't see one."

"It was dark in the hootch," I said. "There was a lot of smoke."

"The dinks always police up the weapons," said Cuda. "They probably went into the ville that night after we pulled out and snatched it away."

"Even so," said Tender, "what about Tuyet? What about the mama-san, the little boy? He knew they wouldn't hurt him. They were family."

Jones sat down next to Tender on the sandbags and rubbed his knee.

"We don't know what happened in there," he said. "None of us do."

"They were like his own family," said Tender.

Jones put his head in his hands and held it there.

"He fucked up all right," he said. "The man went and fucked up real bad. And he be paying for it now for sure. He be paying and paying."

"There had to be a reason," I said.

"Fuckin' reason," said Jones. "It could have been any one of us. That's the reason."

I wanted to be able to argue with him, but all I had were the fragments: the stranger in the hootch, a weapon no one had ever found, the sound of an M-16. The corpses of the woman Neumann loved, her mother, her baby brother, twisted in the dirt. We could have sat there making up stories about them all day, war stories. And if you hadn't been there, hadn't known Neumann and Tuyet, they might have seemed true. We could have said that Tuyet and her family had been VC all along, that they had ambushed him. Except that we knew who they were; Neumann had shown us how to trust them. We could have said that Neumann had just gotten scared, had lashed out wildly in every direction. Except that we had all seen the way he held his fire, the way he handled danger as if he had been born to it. That was the trouble. We knew what we knew, and we didn't know anything more. And so when Jones said that Neumann had fucked up, fucked up bad, nobody could tell him why he was wrong.

There wasn't much cheer as we said our good-byes that day, wished each other luck. The Blues went off on some kind of mission the new LT had cooked up. They moved toward the choppers in a line, and they did not look back at me.

I had to hang around waiting to hitch a ride back to the rear. Apache stayed behind, too. When he found me sitting on my bunk, he took my hand and shook it. I asked him what he thought about what Neumann had done. He replied by handing me one last fragment. He told me who the stranger in the hootch had really been. I could not be angry with Apache. He was only telling me what he had learned, just as he always had. And if the truth had implications, if it meant that Neumann had even less reason to fire, well, we had taught Apache never to shade the facts.

As I took the long plane ride home, I tried to fit that fragment in with the others. But they did not go together, all the jagged edges. And the voices that once had confined themselves to my night-mares now haunted me in the light. They put it all on Neumann. He had gone out in search of who he was. And, baby, he had found it all right. He had touched the rotten center of it. I still believed in Jim Neumann, but it was hard. It was hard.

The plane dipped dramatically as we came in to land. Down below, bright lights lined San Francisco's streets, and the cars moved back and forth like pinballs in a gigantic, gaudy carnival machine. The jet descended; the score mounted up, the numbers that led us home. Then the jet passed into a thin cloud, and suddenly the nightscape became an engulfing web, glistening with dew.

"What'd you expect," said Daniels, "a fuckin' parade?"

Barnelli was polishing his bunged-up belt buckle with an olive-drab handkerchief and not having much success with it. We had been in Oakland for half a day already, and the waiting gave no signs of coming to an end. First there had been a delay. Then there had been papers to sign. Then another delay. An administrative sandwich.

"Not a parade," said Barnelli. "I'm done with being a soldier. But didn't you expect something to happen at the airport?"

"When the plane touched down," I said, "somebody yelled 'Free at last!'"

"I saw who it was," said Daniels. "He was wearing dress greens. One sorry little national defense ribbon on his chest. Stationed in Tokyo, I bet. Free at last. Big fuckin' deal."

"You ever play ball in school?" said Barnelli. "Sometimes, you know, you would go to an away game and really give it everything you had, but you'd still lose. Then you'd shower and get dressed and board the bus. Everybody would be real quiet,

213

and the coach would be up there in the front seat just staring straight ahead at the oncoming traffic, not saying a word. The thing of it was, I never really did feel bad on those rides home, and I don't know if anybody else did either. We just kept quiet because when you lose you think you should."

"That what you think we should do?" said Daniels. "Just shut the fuck up?"

"That ain't it exactly," said Barnelli. "This time I don't even know how we're supposed to feel."

"You keep mostly to yourself," I said to a guy who was sitting near us.

"Sure," he said.

"My name's Morgan."

"I'm Fuentes," he said.

"Why don't you come over and join us? We're all grunts, too."

"I met a lot of guys in the Nam, you know," he said. "Then they were gone."

"You take guys by the minute," I said. "It's all you can count on."

"No real reason anymore," he said.

"The dying's over," I said.

"I guess."

"It takes time," I said. "We aren't a bunch of pigeons. Going home doesn't come natural."

The last physical. We waited in line holding our clothes in front of us in bundles as if we were out-of-town businessmen caught in a raid.

"What did you do, trooper," the doctor said, "sit on a grenade? Funny way to be a hero."

"They say there's still some metal in there," I

said. "They say sometime it will work itself out. Is that right, Doc?"

"Got a case of hemorrhoids, too," he said. "How about your prick?"

"What about it?"

He examined me roughly. "It's clean," he said. "You been a good boy? You hooked, Sergeant? You got a habit?" He looked at my inner elbows and knees, then he peered up my nose.

"I picked up a habit, all right," I said, "but it isn't the kind you're thinking about. Whenever I take a dump, I always turn around to see what kind of mess I've made."

The doctor slapped my shoulder.

"Next," he said.

At the airport Daniels got an early flight. Fuentes, Barnelli and I had a longer wait. The bar looked out over the runways and up the hills of the city, streetlights glittering in the cool, clear night. Barnelli took a deep breath of the tavern's malty air and ran his fingers back and forth along the artificial leather arms of the chair.

"Class," he said.

"May I take your order?" asked the waitress, showing plenty of thigh below a tiny skirt.

"Outasight," said Barnelli.

"Bourbon—double—on the rocks," said Fuentes.

"Same," I said.

"Give me rum and coke," said Barnelli.

"You have ID?" asked the waitress.

"You've got to be kidding," I said.

"Only the little one," she said, pointing at Barnelli.

"He's just back from Vietnam," said Fuentes.

"Got to have proof of age," she said impatiently. "You have it or not?"

"Let's get out of here," said Fuentes.

"Hey," said Barnelli. "It's OK. I'll just have the coke."

"I only follow orders, sweetheart," said the waitress.


We were into our third drink when a wasted little Spec-4 came over to our table. He stood behind Fuentes glassy-eyed, just listening to our bullshit. Fuentes offered him a chair, pulled it out for him. The Spec-4 just stood there smiling. Then he said: "You back from the Place?"

"Roger that," we said, as a man.

The New Guy nodded, grooving on it. His uniform was disheveled. But he didn't seem to care. He carried a battered leather briefcase with a scuffed pair of jungle boots hanging from the handles by the laces. His voice rumbled in his throat.

"You all out for good? ETS?"

"There it is," we said, a chorus.

New Guy reached out his hand. Barnelli grasped it, arm-wrestling style, and squeezed earnestly. Fuentes and I repeated the ritual.

"I'm going back over," New Guy said. His smile had turned crazy. "Third time. I'm going back. Can you dig it?"

We all nodded. He slugged down some more booze, shook off the shock of it, then went into a rap.

"I tried the World for a while, really. I mean, I actually tried it on for size. You dig, man? I tried

216

it. Dig?" Fuentes gave a little gesture that put his needle back in the track.

"Like I was stationed at Bliss. Man, don't go down to Bliss. Don't *even* go down there, man. Dig? Like I was down there in the heat, man. The barracks and inspections and the assholes and everything. I'm back from the Nam and stuck in Bliss."

Barnelli had gotten into a nodding routine to keep New Guy going.

"Then they cut me orders back to the Nam," he continued. "They decided to send me back to the Place. . . .

"Man, you'll hate it here. I tried the World, man. Like I really gave it a chance. You'll hate it, the World."

He talked in spirals, picking up speed as the curves narrowed in. I followed him down.

"You'll groove for a little while, sure. I did. But then you'll hate it."

"Look at that chick over there," said Fuentes, trying to pull the guy out of the spin. "She got that look. She wants me, but she don't know how to ask."

"Sure, you'll dig the chicks for a while. My bitch, my old lady, she and I do the good thing, man. I mean, we get it on. But we got other things cookin', too. She does her thing. I do mine. Sometimes we get it together. And now they're sending me back to the Place, and I won't *even* have to see that filthy bitch again."

I touched his shoulder to calm him. He flinched.

"I don't care if I do go back to the Place. I mean, I'm gone already. I never left. Dig it? I'm not going because I'm already gone. Man, don't you understand? I got to do it now, before I'm dead. And so I got all my records. They'll never fuckin' find me. I'm gone. You dig? I'm going. So I'm gone."

"Hey, look," said Fuentes. "We got to split now. Get some dinner, you know?"

"No, man," New Guy pleaded. "Have one more for the Place, man."

"Eating's my thing right now," said Fuentes.

"OK, man. But you're not going to hack it back here. Take it from me. Once you been gone, you can't *ever* come back. I tried and now I got to go."

"Easy," said Fuentes, taking his hand. It startled him, then he settled back.

Barnelli finally caught his flight after dinner. The plane eased slowly away from the gate. We waited until it took off and then waited some more. A big blond Spec-4 without a nameplate joined us. He just sort of appeared next to Fuentes and me as we stood at the gate. When we didn't seem to have anything to say, it turned out that he did.

He offered up the fact right away that he had been a grunt in the 4th Infantry Division and had seen a lot of trouble at LZ Phillips in Cambodia. I had heard of it, and it was nothing to bullshit about. The brass had planned to insert a battalion, but they only got part of a company in before the NVA started popping choppers out of the air. After an hour, all the officers were dead. The grunts sat in the middle of an NVA base camp and had to fight for a fingerhold for twenty-four hours. The Spec-4 admitted without being asked that those twenty-four hours had screwed him up plenty. He finally introduced himself.

"Call me Kent State," he said, because that was where he had gone to school. Knew the kids who got greased on campus, too, he volunteered. He was all the time looking back and forth at Fuentes and me as he spoke, seeing what we registered. We felt we ought to accept him, I suppose, like kin. But there was something peculiar about him for a grunt. He didn't wear a combat infantry badge.

"Like I was on the ground getting shot up, you know," he said, "and when it let up they brought in the *Stars and Stripes*. There it was, the kids at Kent State had been wasted by the National Guard."

"Four KIA," I said. "Big fucking deal."

"You a lifer?" asked Kent State.

"Going home, just like you."

"You talk like a lifer," he said. "You're gonna have to learn what it's like back in the World. Nobody believes in that GI Joe shit anymore. Face it, we were on the wrong side."

"It didn't have sides," I said. "No beginning, no end."

"That guy in the bar," said Fuentes. "He was pretty bad. Speed and booze, I bet. Some guys get that way. They take a hit for fun, then it gets bad. I think he just wanted to talk. Maybe we shouldn't have left him."

"I think he'll be OK," I said, "when he gets wherever the hell he thinks he's going."

"Just like us," said Fuentes. "Let's walk." And we did, the three of us.

Near a stationery counter, a big Buffalo Bill of a

219

guy with long, dirty hair, a thin beard and a tasseled buckskin coat stopped us. With him was a little Botticelli of a girl, maybe eighteen, with a round, pale face and curly red hair.

"You have any spare change?" Buffalo Bill asked.

"Sorry," said Kent State, though you could hear it jingling in his pocket.

I reached for a couple of quarters.

"Wait," said Buffalo Bill. "I shouldn't even ask you guys. You've been ripped off enough already. Back from the Nam, right?"

We all nodded, in perfect cadence.

"Wow," breathed Buffalo Bill. His girl kept her passive smile. "Going home?"

We nodded again.

"Wow."

The loudspeaker called a flight and we all listened up as if it were the CO in the command chopper giving us our orders.

"Let it be when you get home," said Buffalo Bill. "Just let it be."

He turned away.

"Hold on," said Fuentes. "You in trouble?"

"No, man," said Buffalo Bill. "Just a car without gas and a taste for a hit in San Jose, that's all. No trouble. No bread is all."

Fuentes pulled out his wallet and took from it a freshly ironed ten-dollar bill.

"Here," he said. "Take it and make it in San Jose."

"Wow," said Buffalo Bill, turning it in his hand to show the girl, as if it were a piece of fine tapestry. She nearly grinned.

"I can't take it," he said. "It's too much. All I wanted was some change."

"It's OK," said Fuentes, softly. "Just got paid. I know what having no bread is. Just drop a cap for me."

That gave Kent State an idea. He sidled up to Buffalo Bill and whispered conspiratorially in his ear.

"Sorry," said Buffalo Bill. "I don't have any shit on me. The only shit I know of is where I'm going. If I had any, I'd give it to you. Really. Want to come along?"

Kent State brushed back a shock of hair.

"Man," he said, "I got hit bad in the Nam, and I got hooked to beat the pain. I gotta have some shit."

"I'd like to help," said Buffalo Bill, "but I just don't have any with me."

"OK," said Kent State, and dropped it.

Funny thing for a guy with a wound, he didn't wear a ribbon for the Purple Heart, only a few bullshit service medals.

"I can't take this money," said Buffalo Bill with determination.

"Look," said Fuentes, just as firmly. "Just take it and go. We're all celebrating here. The end of the war, right?"

"OK, man. Thanks. Really. Peace at last. I don't fucking believe it."

"Neither do I," said Fuentes. "But celebrate anyway, OK?"

As they walked away from us, Kent State began to describe in clinical detail the precise shape of his need.

"First it was opium joints," he said. "But then out in the bad bush I graduated to the hard way. Mainline, baby."

"Grunts don't shoot dope," I said. "Nobody goes into the bush with somebody stoned out of his mind."

"Man," said Kent State, "you and me must of been in different wars."

"They're all the same," I said.

"Only some are bigger," said Fuentes.

Kent State led us on a rangy recon mission through the terminal. His need included, he said, "a little round-eye snatch."

"That one over there," he said. "She's got a nice face but bad wheels, bad."

Then: "Too old, but a nice body. I like them fresh."

Then: "Well, hello, sweet thing. Why don't you give me a call in a few years when you get legal."

Finally, he spotted two college girls in sweaters and jeans. Very nice. Long, straight hair. California tans.

"You're more beautiful," he said, "than coming home alive."

"We're not available," said the taller one.

"I'm sorry," said Kent State. "I didn't mean to come on to you. I apologize. In the jungle you forget how to behave."

"I bet," said the shorter girl.

"I just got home from the Nam," said Kent State, "and it's been a long time since I saw a woman I could relate to."

"We meant no harm," said Fuentes. "We didn't mean to scare you."

"Oh, you didn't scare anybody," said the tall one, running her hand through her hair, then shaking her head so the hair cascaded and billowed to drive a man crazy.

"They say," said the shorter one, "they say we burn villages and kill women and children over there."

Fuentes snickered.

"They say there are atrocities," she said.

"Helen!"

"No, really," said Kent State. "I understand. Well, I saw some . . . some pretty bad things, I guess."

"Do you want to talk about them?" said the taller one, softening.

"It isn't easy," said Kent State, edging them slowly toward some empty chairs. "It turned me all inside out. It messed me up. I don't know."

"If you'd rather not . . ." But by then they had gotten all comfortable, and Kent State was ready.

"We were going through a little village," he said softly, and the two girls leaned close so they could hear every awful word. "It was in the Central Highlands. We were going through this town, the whole company. And the people all went inside their hootches. The guys were pretty mad because a couple of us got hit the day before. But these were just women and old people and little children. They hadn't done anything to us, you know? But one of the sergeants said, 'Let's have a little party.' And so, well, we got all the people out of their hootches and lined them up. There were maybe twenty of them. And one of the little kids gave the sergeant the finger. Well, he was only maybe six or seven years old. He probably didn't even know what it meant. But when the guys saw that they . . ."

Kent State paused, swallowed, waited. Perfect timing.

"Don't be afraid," said the taller one.

"They were all dead," said Kent State. "Killed them all."

"It's just like My Lai!" said the shorter one.

"You killed them? I mean, just killed them?" said the taller one.

"I didn't kill anybody," said Kent State. "I fired in the air. I swear it."

"It must have been just horrible," said the taller one. "I'm so sorry."

"Balls," I said.

"That's just what you'd expect," said the taller one, glaring at me. "That's the attitude that made it all happen."

Fuentes took me aside as the two girls consoled Kent State.

"He can't help it," said Fuentes. "Sure it's bullshit. He probably wasn't even a grunt."

"He's as phony as a body count."

"Don't be blaming him too much, though," said Fuentes. "Something happened to him over there. Something went wrong. He's just trying to find a way to make people listen is all."

"He's trying to get laid."

"Maybe so," said Fuentes. "But he wants people to know how it was. We all do. And he's afraid they wouldn't listen to the truth even if he could get it together to give it to them. I feel bad for him. Real bad."

"You know it was never as simple as he said."

"Some people," said Fuentes, "they die a little bit at a time. And pride goes first, man. Pride is easy to kill."

My folks met me at the airport with a jeroboam of champagne. My mother hugged me, kissed me on the lips. My father embraced me, too. One or two of the other passengers stopped and smiled at us, but most of them just walked on by.

I wanted to open the bottle right there and take a swig. I wanted to pass it around, hand to hand, a ritual. But my father was nervous. They probably had rules, he said, eyeing the ticket agent. And anyway, it was barely dawn. It was just too early, he said.

He tried to carry my duffel bag for me, but it was too heavy, so I hefted it to my shoulder and we marched to the car. I remembered how on the first day of basic training, the drill sergeants had made us lug the bag along wherever we went, how my shoulders had sagged. The trick was in the balance. You had to kind of lean into it. It wasn't nearly as awkward as carrying the dead weight of a man.

The noise of the car engine and the wind sealed me off from them as we drove the expressways home. I gazed out at all the old places. They were familiar but at the same time they seemed some- how changed. It was like coming out of a black and white movie into the sun and being amazed that the world came in colors.

I dozed a little in the backseat, but I woke up when we reached our street. They had repainted the house. I told them how nice it looked as we bounced into the driveway.

"You've planted new hedges, too," I said.

"We've been getting ready for this day for months," said my mother.

Something melancholy inside of me wanted out. I stemmed it.

"I've been counting the days, too," I said be- cause it was a literal fact. You could not go wrong sticking to the truth, the fragments. For now you just had to keep it simple, coming home. We weren't pigeons. It wasn't second nature to us.

The house smelled just the way it always had. My father's pipe tobacco, my mother's favorite spices, the clean, rich mix of furniture polish, flowers, heavy drapes. I would have known it blind.

"We've moved things around since you left," said my mother. "Do you still recognize it?"

Beethoven glared at me from over the piano. A sliver of sun through a part in the drapes drew a thin, light skewline across the dark carpet. I could have told time by the angle of that line.

"It looks fine," I said.

"I'll get us some breakfast," said my mother.

"We'll build a fire if you'd like. You must be unaccustomed to the cold."

"I'd better get out of this uniform," I said, holding the lapels out with two fingers of each hand, as if it were something diseased. "We can use it for kindling."

"Oh, don't throw it away, Bill," my mother said. "Don't you remember your father's old coat and stripes? You used to like to play with them, put them on. Someday your children will want to do the same with yours."

I did not argue with her. Facts. Literal facts. I just went to my room and dropped the heavy clothes off into a heap. I found my frayed old robe and wrapped it around me, a touch of the past. The red dirt came out of my hair as I showered. The water splashed pink at my feet, pink and muddy like the water in the washbowl when you give yourself a good gash shaving, like the creek in Xuan The where they showed me the bodies.

No. Nothing like that. It was all right now. Everything was all right. Everything.

At breakfast my mother was already making plans.

"Your aunts want to come by to see you very soon," she said as I struggled to tame the crude way I shoveled my food into my mouth and puzzled over the forgotten etiquette of grapefruit.

"I bet you haven't had fresh fruit in a long time," said my father.

"Kids sold papayas and bananas," I said. "Stuff grew wild." Fact.

"Your aunts are so proud of you," said my mother.

"What for?"

"Well, they talk about you all the time. I showed them your letters. They think you're pretty special."

"I like them, too," I said.

"There were so few your age who accepted the responsibility," said my mother.

"You do what you have to do," I said, which was my way of absolving everyone. But my father did not take it that way.

"Absolutely," he said. "When the call comes, you honor it. Duty. They will come to regret what they did someday."

"John Russell was over in Vietnam," said my mother. "Do you remember him?"

"The name," I said. "Sure. John Russell. He was a year or two behind me, I think."

"He was killed there," my mother said softly.

"Fuckit," I said.

When I looked up and saw their faces, I realized what I had said, not only the word but the way it sounded, and I was sorry.

My mother folded and unfolded the napkin next to her plate.

"I shouldn't have mentioned it," she said. "I thought maybe you knew already."

"It's all right," I said.

I went on to glut myself on eggs and pastry. I asked for seconds. My parents didn't seem to have much of an appetite. They let the food go cold on their plates. I figured that they must have eaten something before going to meet my plane.

I spent that first day pretty much to myself. I unloaded all the junk from my duffel, sorting it out—the boots, the uniforms, the souvenirs, the R and R clothes, the letters I had saved. Then I went through my room picking up old things, just holding them in my hand. There were yearbooks from school. I flipped through them for the pictures of old girlfriends, pictures of myself. I looked up John Russell, and there he was, hair swept back in a greasy DA. I remembered him. He was one of the guys who always hung around the woodshop door, smelling of hand tools and smoke. He used to get into fights, and he was pretty good with his fists, the poor dumb bastard.

In the closet I came across an old cigar box wrapped around with rubber bands and twine. It wasn't exactly where I had left it. Nothing was. But it didn't look like it had been tampered with. My mother had moved things around, organizing them. I pictured her doing it while I was away, busy as hell, not allowing herself any tears.

I pulled the bindings off the box and looked inside. It held all the things I had put aside in my rush to go off to the army. An old package of condoms that I didn't know what to do with that last day. Some photographs of Sharon and the necklace I had given her and she had felt obliged to return. I thought I had thrown that damned thing away. And at the bottom was a sealed envelope containing the message I had written to them in case I was killed. I did not even read it over. It embarrassed me, and I threw it away.

But I could not as easily rid myself of the feeling that I was not alone, that a double was shadowing me, looking over my shoulder, taking stock. When my parents glanced my way, they measured me against him. The pictures on the wall, in the yearbooks, they had his face. I could not really see him, but he was there. I knew him from his whispered voice. *Welcome home, soldier boy. Did you think I had gone away?* It was the ghost of my younger self. I had changed. I had been propelled by the green. And he had stayed the same. There was no way to make the connection between the two. We were separate, and he haunted me.

That evening before dinner I went into the bathroom to clean up. I forgot to shut the door. I stripped off my shirt and looked into the mirror. Still a fucking grunt. My father was watching me from the hall.

"Come on in," I said.

"You're looking mighty good," he said. "They hardened you up some."

He could not see the scars.

"Mom's cooking will take care of that," I said.

"I just want to tell you that I think you've come through this whole difficult business very strong."

I looked away from him, caught my angry eyes in the mirror. I breathed in, then out halfway, the way they taught you to do before pulling the trigger, to steady your aim.

"They put a lot of years on this old face," I said, touching the sun-baked flesh.

"Maturity," he said. "Growing up."

It wasn't until after dinner that I thought to ask about the dog. I hadn't heard him barking. When I asked, my parents' faces suddenly grew long.

"Let's go to the other room, son," said my father. "Your mother will want to clean up here."

I followed him into the den, where he sat me down in his big reclining chair.

"I guess something happened to Sparky," I said. "Is that it?"

"He was very sick," my father said slowly, and then he laid it all out from the beginning, which was his way. "I don't know what exactly it was. Some condition of the heart. He was pretty old."

I counted the years. I had been twelve when we got him, a tiny mongrel pup saved from the gas chamber at the pound. They had decided that I was old enough to learn a sense of responsibility.

"I took him to the vet when it got bad. That must have been six months ago now. We didn't want to write you about it. You had enough on your mind. The vet said it was hopeless. There was nothing we could do."

His voice faltered. He looked away from me, and his eyes were damp. It was ridiculous, really. Both of us. I felt a catch in my throat and I was blinking too much. But, I mean, it was just a sick old dog.

"We had to put him to sleep," he said. "It was the only thing we could do."

I stood up and put my arm around his shoulder. "It's OK," I said. "It's OK."

That night I was ready to sleep like a stone. I hadn't gotten more than a couple hours at a stretch since I climbed aboard the *Freedom Bird*, and so I turned in early.

My mother had laid out my pajamas, folded neatly and squared away with the corner of the bunk. But it didn't feel right putting them on, something about the fabric, the feel of it against my skin. I got back into my olive-drab underwear and crawled between the covers. I turned out the light.

There were noises. Traffic on the highway. The hum of the furnace. Muffled television from my parents' room down the hall, laughter. I closed my eyes. The bed was soft as mud. As I squirmed to my belly, to my back, I couldn't help feeling that I was sinking in too deep. The window was open, but the room was stifling, confined. My muscles were tense and twitching. A fist clenched in my gut. With my eyes closed, I thought I heard footsteps, cracking twigs, the rustle of leaves after the wind died down. I put my hand out to touch the cold metal of my rifle, but of course it was not there. All the whiskey I had consumed did not even touch my excited nerves. I wished I had some of that strong dope they had given me in the hospital.

When I finally heard the television go off, I counted out a full ten minutes before rolling from the bed. I dressed in the dark and stole out as quietly as I could. All the lights in the house were off, but my night vision was still very good. I tested each board before stepping on it. I did not make a sound. In the bush the whole damned platoon of Blues could move through the jungle as silent as a snake. It was easy, when you had to.

Downstairs I put on my boots and field jacket. It was pretty cold outside, so I brought a couple of blankets with me before making my way to the garage. Luckily, the door was open. I didn't want to have to put out a window to get in. Dog smells still hung in the damp air. We always kept him outside because he was half wild and restless in tighter quarters. I lit a match.

Someone had ripped out the little bed my father and I had made for the dog and had scrubbed the whole place down. My father's tools hung in orderly rows on a pegboard over the work bench, arranged by function and size. I could see my breath burst in a cloud as I blew out the match. I would have brought a candle, but you never knew whether someone would notice it and become concerned. Light discipline. I waited until my eyes got used to the shadows again, then I put down the blankets and went outside. My fingers searched out a soft piece of earth with no leaves. I got down on my knees, unzipped and pissed in perfect silence.

Poor old dog, I thought as I went back into the garage and spread a blanket in a corner that commanded all the windows and the door. He would have known me, no matter how much I had changed. They were sharp that way, a keen sense of identity, something wild in the nostrils. They could always tell friends from enemies. It was a saving instinct, in the wilds.

The concrete floor was hard and cold, but I relaxed on it. I shivered a little at first, but no more than on cold nights in the bush. At least I was dry. I pulled the other blankets tight around me like a poncho and liner and settled down. I was asleep in a matter of minutes, and I did not awaken and return to my room until first light.

The one obligation still before me was to report to the Veterans' Administration. If you want to be sure you get a proper burial, the officer in Oakland had said, you got to get your ass down there and get your card. I put it off at first; I just didn't have the energy. Then one day I finally borrowed my father's car and set off. It drove a lot mushier than the jeeps I was used to. I did not like the power steering or the hair-trigger brakes. You lost the good feeling of rutted earth beneath the tires.

There were long lines at the VA, but I didn't mind them. We traded stories, exchanged the names of our units, the places in Cambodia we had seen. There were quite a few who had never left the States. They stayed to themselves, giving us looks. Somebody made a crack about their masculinity.

The lady typed up my card, explained all the good benefits, especially if I wanted to buy a house, go back to school, get sick or die. I tried to listen. But the only thing that really registered was when she told me about the unemployment pay.

"You're out of a job, aren't you?" she said.

"Sure. You have any listings for Eleven Bravos?"

I kind of liked her, even though she did not seem to know how to smile.

"There's a special program for returning vets," she said. "Pays benefits with no questions asked so long as you haven't taken work."

"Not much chance of that," I said.

"You can take the money or not," she said. "If I were you, I'd take whatever I could get. Swallow your pride."

I gulped. It went down like a tiny little pea. I grinned.

"And don't forget to file for your Illinois bonus."

"Bonus?"

"A little welcome-home check. Thank you for a job well done."

"I guess they haven't been reading the papers."

"Look," she said. "You have a good record here. You don't have anything to apologize for."

"I'm sorry," I said. "I wasn't apologizing."

My father was horrified that I had gone on the dole. The state bonus business was apparently all right. It was like a tax break, I suppose, as opposed to welfare. If I needed money, he said, why didn't I just ask him? He even offered to go out and buy me a car.

"I appreciate that, Dad," I said. "I really do. But I don't think I want to get loaded down with things right now. I'm traveling light."

"Have you thought about what you're going to do?"

"Yes, indeed," I said. "I've been thinking about that a lot."

Somehow we managed to leave it there.

But the trouble was that I had no idea where to go from here. I spent days just sitting in my room, waiting for something to come along and make me move. Inertia had me, dead weight and fatigue. I would go through the things I had brought back with me, the photographs of the Blues clowning around for somebody's new lens, the postcards from Tokyo, the brass Montagnard bracelet they said would save your life. I read and reread the letter from Neumann that had come the day after I arrived home. There was no return address.

"I'm sorry for the way I acted at the inquiry," it

said. "But I knew what all of you were thinking, and you were wrong. Maybe I should have had it in me to set you straight, but I didn't. Let's let the war be over, OK? Let's leave it alone."

If Neumann didn't want to see me, then I had nowhere to go at all. And so I just sat there picking up things, pieces of paper, pictures, the little brass shell casings and black fragments I liked to turn over and over in my hand.

At night I would sometimes go out cruising around in my father's car. At first I went to neighboring suburbs to do my drinking. I wanted to be sure I would not be known. I would pick out a bar, a nice place with dark laminated tables and rich mock-leather booths, and find a spot in the remotest corner. I did not drink heavily, because I knew it didn't do any good. I would nurse a few beers for as long as I could, watching whatever the bartender had chosen on the TV.

After a while I grew bold enough to stay in town. Usually, it didn't matter. Maybe there were a few faces at the bar that I thought I should have known, but nobody recognized me.

Then one night, as I was sitting alone at the back of Larry's Tap, a group of my high school classmates came in. I moved farther back in the booth, blew out the little candle on the table and hid my face behind my glass until they got settled at the bar. Then I heaved myself out of my booth and hurried past them.

"Bill Morgan," said a woman's voice. "Is that Bill Morgan? You've lost weight. You look so good."

I should not have paused. I should have left the name behind.

"What the hell have you been doing with yourself?" said one of the men. It was Gary Plunkett. He used to have a mean turnaround jump shot. "You back in town now?"

"Here I am," I said, and I felt like a fool.

"Nice tan," said Richard Watkins, shaking my hand. Every winter when we were in school, he would come back from Christmas vacation and show off in the locker room, the contrast between his arm and his ass. It's funny what you remember.

"You sure didn't get that tan in this town," said Danny Pike, slapping me on the back and giving my shoulder a little massage.

"I've been away."

"You remember my wife, Sherry," said Plunkett.

"Of course," I said. She was the one who had recognized me trying to sneak away. "I didn't realize you were married. Congratulations."

"Here," said Pike. "Sit down. Have a drink."

"I really have to be going."

"What are you drinking anyway?"

"Beer," I said. "Just beer." I did not want to stay, but I didn't know how to get away. I hovered there like a chopper half off its skids.

"Bring this man a brew."

I leaned up against the edge of an empty stool and took a sip when the bartender put the glass before me. I tried to pay, but Plunkett motioned for the man to take it out of the pile of crumpled bills next to his cigarettes on the bar.

"You hear from any of the old crowd?" he said.

"I've been sort of out of touch."

"Jay Siegle's working downtown in the trust section of the First National," said Pike.

"You remember Bob Johnson?" asked Randolph.

"I guess," I said.

"He's about to become a doctor."

"What are you doing these days?" asked Plunkett.

"Not much."

"Don't tell me you're loafing. You used to be a grind."

"Just got out of the army," I said.

"No shit," said Randolph.

"Well, that at least explains the haircut," said Pike, mussing up what little had grown back on my head. I pulled back from the touch, tensed up. Everyone saw it. Pike drew away; the silly sonofabitch must have thought I wanted to fight.

"Somebody else was in the army," said Randolph, breaking the uncomfortable silence. "Who the hell was it now?"

"Where were you stationed?" asked Sherry.

"Vietnam," I said.

"How did it happen?" she asked, so very earnestly, as if there had been some terrible traffic accident.

"The usual way," I said, trying to get the smile just right.

"I mean, did you actually have to . . ."

"Fight?" I said. "Once in a while. I was in the infantry."

"How long were you over there?"

"A year," I said. "The tour of duty is a year." I thought everybody knew at least that much.

"They draft your ass?" asked Watkins.

"Sure did."

"Christ," said Plunkett. "I still remember the day I had to go downtown to take my physical."

"You were so concerned," said Sherry, taking his arm.

"I ended up staying awake for seventy-two hours," said Pike, "drinking coffee to get my blood pressure up. Guy who finally took it told me I ought to check right into the hospital."

"Sometimes I wonder, though," said Plunkett when they stopped laughing, "whether maybe I didn't miss something. You know, an experience. Something to tell the kids about."

"If we raise them right, they'll understand," said Sherry.

"My old man was in World War Two," said Pike. "His stories are just the same old bullshit."

"Maybe you ought to listen to them," I said. "Maybe he's still got something on his mind."

They waited a moment, all of them, looking at me as if I had spoken out of turn.

"If my boys turn out anything like me," said Watkins, "they won't be cut out for it. Some guys are and some guys aren't."

"You might be surprised at what you can do if you have to," I said. My hand was wrapped so tightly around the beer mug that it was beginning to ache.

"I've got this problem with taking orders," he said.

"That's the easy part," I said.

The conversation stopped then as we all took our bearings. I did not want to challenge what they had done any more than they wanted to challenge what I had done. But these things hung like a foul odor between us. They did not have to be spoken.

"It must have been terrible for you," Sherry said finally.

"Hey, thanks for the beer," I said, looking at my watch. "It's getting late. I really have to go."

"We ought to get together sometime," said Plunkett, grabbing my hand and giving it a convincing shake. "The whole gang."

"Let's do it," said Pike.

But nobody tried to stop me from going, and I was glad of it.

As I left, I overheard Randolph's voice, a little thick with whiskey and probably louder than he really wanted it to be.

"I don't know what comes over these guys," he said. "They get to be a real pain in the ass."


My father was still up when I got home. He was reading in the den, and he caught me trying to slip past the door.

"Bill?"

I stepped in, and he put down the book. It was some old thing by James Jones.

"You had a call tonight. Richard Herring. Didn't you have him here for a weekend one time?"

"Years ago," I said.

"He left a number where you could reach him tomorrow. I put it on the corkboard above the phone."

"Thanks." I made a move to leave.

"Do you have a minute?" he asked. I looked at my watch. I had to laugh. He laughed, too.

"I suppose I could spare it."

"I was wondering whether there was anything I could do for you," he said.

"Do?"

"Whether you wanted to talk out the possibilities. Maybe I could get in touch with people at the university. Or if you wanted, I could scope out what kind of positions are available downtown."

"Why don't you hold off for a while," I said.

"Is there something bothering you, son?"

"Just a little tired, that's all," I said. "Catching my breath. You know how it is. I'll be all right."

"You let me know if there's anything you want," he said.

"I'll let you know."

I was pretty slow about calling Richard the next day. Little things kept coming up that delayed me: My shoes were scuffed, and I gave them a professional spit shine that took more than an hour. The books on my shelves had gotten out of order. I rearranged them all, first by subject, and then, when that did not please me, by author's name.

But when I did get around to dialing Richard's number and heard his cool, crazy voice asking me to meet him in the city, I practically dropped the phone and ran to the car. He could be a little strange sometimes, but I thought maybe he just might be able to understand. I was feeling pretty strange myself.

The place where he wanted me to meet him was in Old Town. When I pulled into Wells Street, it seemed a lot different from the way I had remembered it in the days when we used to go down there on Saturday nights and listen to the folk music and eat the spicy ethnic food. The buildings seemed crowded together now, kind of dingy and run-down, and there were adult bookstores and gaudy tourist traps squatting among the renovated places. It used to be a carnival on the streets, everybody friendly, talking to each other. But that day the people walked under umbrellas in the light rain, eyes to the ground. They did not look at one another as they passed.

I traded the car for a claim check and heard the garage attendant burning rubber on the ramp as I hit the street. The restaurant where I was supposed to meet Richard was up the way, just a little hamburger joint. I took a booth near the back, ordered a cup of coffee and waited. Most of the people at the counter and tables were young. They dressed in all kinds of costumes. Headbands, beads, bib overalls, even field jackets and boots. I could tell by the length of the men's hair that they had not been away across the pond. Yet still they all seemed sullen and depressed. I could not understand it. I wanted to go up to one of them, take him by the lapels and tell him how goddamned happy he should be. I did not do it, of course. The last thing I needed was to draw attention to myself.

Finally, Richard arrived. He was wearing a rumpled button-down shirt, droopy sports jacket, khaki pants. You almost expected to see a briefcase in his hand, he looked so straight. But if you knew him, you realized that this was a measure of his eccentricity. He simply never noticed that he did not look like everyone else around him.

"Billy Morgan, boy hero," he said, laughing. I wouldn't have taken that from anybody but Richard, but I remembered his regular letters, remembered how he had spent time with me during the weeks before I was drafted, the days before I went overseas. I owed him one. More than one. I stood up at the booth and we embraced like kin.

"How long have you been back?" he said when we sat down.

"Few weeks."

"Why the hell didn't you call me?"

I took a long breath. I wasn't sure it was going to work, but I wanted to try to be straight with him.

"I guess I might have been scared," I said.

"A case of post-traumatic-stress syndrome," he said. If a thing had a name, you could always count on Richard to know it.

"It isn't a disease," I said. I could feel myself pulling back already.

"Don't shrivel up on me here," he said.

"I've had trouble talking about it." I waited for a minute before deciding to risk it. "I've been having this dream."

"Keep going," he said. "You're doing fine."

"It isn't such a bad dream, really. Nothing happens to me. I'm just kind of watching."

"And what do you see?"

"There are people in the dream who say it could have been different. I deny it. But they say they'll show me how. Then they never do. They're dead people, Richard. They taunt me, but the dream always ends too soon. I'd like just one time to see how they think it could have come out otherwise."

"You're holding back," said Richard. "You aren't going to shock me."

"Maybe I wish I could."

"Why don't you try?"

I stretched my fingers out long on the Formica tabletop to settle the tension that was fluttering there. I tried to work the relaxation up my arms and into my shoulders.

"There was a guy I knew over there," I said. "We were very close, like brothers. I believed in him. But then one day he did something, and it's been fucking me up ever since trying to figure out why."

"Is this guy somebody I know?"

"You don't know him."

"Somebody I know like a brother?"

"I'm not talking about me."

"Any way you want it," he said. "What exactly did this guy do?"

I did not appreciate being humored that way. And so I put it as harshly as I could, just to shake him up.

"He fell in love with a Vietnamese family," I said. "Then he blew them away."

Richard did not show the slightest twinge. It was as if he expected nothing better of a brother of mine, or of me.

"It's that kind of war," he said.

"Listen to what you're saying, Richard. Do you think we all became butchers?"

My voice was getting loud. People were turning around to look at us. I stopped myself, settled down in the booth.

"OK," said Richard. "Fair enough. The guy went bad. It happens here. It happened there. You were wrong about him, that's all."

"I wasn't wrong about him," I said. "If I could just talk to him, I know he could explain why it had to happen the way it did."

"I think maybe you need some help," he said, standing up, and I thought for a moment that I had driven him away. But then he grabbed my coat and pulled me up out of the booth. "Come on over to my place. It isn't far. I've got something I want to show you. Maybe it will bring things together."

I had no idea what he had in mind, and I didn't really care. I was ready to try anything. And so I let him lead the way.

The sun was coming out from behind the clouds. The streets were aswarm. Everyone wore some kind of costume. Street sellers with belts and jewelry were setting up their stands. Suddenly, I had the weird idea that it was all a masquerade, that a chime would ring the hour and all the people on the street would take off their silks and saris and overalls and panama hats to reveal the flat-topped boys and bouffanted girls of high school. Or Davis and Weisman and Jackpot and Tuyet . . .

A horn blared. I jumped.

"Christ," said Richard.

"Reflex," I said. "They say that after a while the noises stop bothering you."

"You looked like you were ready to shoot somebody."

"No sweat," I said. "I'm staying away from guns."

His doorway was in the narrow space between two topless joints. We walked up the creaky stairs.

"Did I ever write you about the I Ching?" Richard asked over his shoulder. "It's Chinese. Yin and yang. Maybe you came across it over there."

"It was a very common symbol," I said. I thought about the figures on the Tet calendar in Tuyet's hootch, the sticks of incense and the stink of the paddies.

"Yin and yang," he said. "Eternal opposites. Ebbs and flows. Masculine and feminine. Heat and cold. One dominates for a time and then it declines. The I Ching reads the changes. It tells you about the circumstances of the future."

He unlocked his door and led me into a large apartment. It was done up with exotic posters and drawings. The bed was a mattress on the floor, a parody of the Japanese. There were brass bowls and icons on the low tables.

"Sit down on the mat," he said, pulling from the shelf a little book wrapped in black silk. He opened it reverently and showed it to me. It was bound in bright cloth like a best seller. He put it down and then stacked on top of it three odd-looking brass coins he dug out of his pocket.

"I don't need to know the future," I said. "I need to know the past. It's like the shrapnel in my ass. Fragments. Facts. I have to connect them up somehow."

"Trust me," he said. "This will help. The Chinese were really onto something."

How many times had I watched Richard's demonstrations, listened to his strange lectures? I used to think it was amusing, the utter enthusiasm with which he invested each new brainstorm. But this time I felt his excitement cutting me off. I watched him as he picked up the coins, threw them, made a notation, threw them again.

"Games of chance," I said.

"I won't explain the process now," he said. "That will come later. For now you can just watch. Go with it. The ritual. The spirit of the thing."

He threw the coins again and again. They jingled on the mat like the little wind chimes that hung from the eaves of pagodas.

"Far out," he said. "Look at this."

He drew two figures on a piece of paper:

```
_____    _____         _____    _____
_____           _____    _____
_____    _____         _____
_____    _____         _____
_____           _____
_____           _____
```

"The first hexagram is *Chun*," he said, "the symbol of birth and its pains. The second hexagram is *T'ai*. Heaven and earth are in close communion, and it is the symbol of peace. Can you see the significance?"

He took up the book.

"The first hexagram is in the process of changing into the second," he said, "and the lines of change are told. Let me read from the commentary on *Chun*. You must listen carefully. You must open yourself to the pure, irrational truth of it. This is straight Confucius:

" 'The start of a new venture is always accompanied by struggles and difficulty. . . .' You see. You see. It is a time for overcoming disorder, for looking ahead. Just like I told you."

"You don't really believe in this stuff, do you?"

"There is also a warning," he said, pointing to

the diagram, running his finger slowly over the broken lines. "Six in the third place. 'He hunts deer without the help of a forester and finds himself lost in the middle of a forest. The superior man, aware of the risk he is courting, chooses to give up the chase. To go forward would bring regret.' "

I thought of Neumann's tale of the hunter and the bear. Parables. All the superstitions we had in the bush. How little any of it helped. I felt anger rising in me, and I suddenly wanted to get away.

"Can you see the significance? The guy you were telling me about," he said, "forget him. Let everything go."

For a moment I thought he was making me the butt of a joke. But when I caught his eye I could see that he was as serious as he could be.

"Richard, this isn't going to work."

"Nine in the fifth place. 'Correct action will ensure good fortune in small things, but in great matters it will lead to disaster.' "

"Do they have a hexagam for carrion?"

"*Ku*," he said. "It is not your sign."

"How about one for somebody who killed the wrong people?"

"Whatever you did, you have to put it behind you now," he said. "Your symbols are birth and peace. There is pain, but there is also the possibility of order."

"Three coins," I said.

I took them off the mat and shook them in my fist like dice. I threw them hard into the corner. They clattered on the wooden floor.

Richard looked over at me as if I had struck him

a blow. He moved on his hands and knees to retrieve the little pieces of metal. And when I went to help him, he pushed me away.

During the next few weeks I spent a lot of time walking, just walking. Up and down the neighborhood streets, looking at the familiar old houses, wondering how behind the warm yellow glow of their windows anyone could go on as if nothing had changed. I went to the woods on the other side of the highway and wandered there alone in the cold. I saw the trees where once I had stood lookout, the narrow places in the creek that were the best spots for a bridge. I hoped that somewhere, somehow, I would begin to feel the sweet tug of my youth. But the force was all in the other direction, pulling me back to where I had grown old.

I paced my room, the door closed against everyone. And I heard them talking. They were worried about when I would get beyond the experience. But I knew that I could never outdistance it. Even if I managed to get it behind me, it would not be very far. It was a shadow, lengthening out with the dusk. I moved. I turned. And there it was, my shape, distorted.

One evening when I came in to dinner, I found at my place at the table a big, brown official envelope. It sat there neatly, next to the knife and spoons, perfectly square with the corner. I picked it up and tossed it under my chair.

"What's that, son?" my father asked.

"Beats me," I said. The thing was bulky and stiff. The safest way to deal with it was to put it aside.

"It may be important," he said. "You'd better open it."

I leaned over and picked it up, slit the paper flap with my dinner knife. Inside was a padded green plastic case with the army seal on it. I opened the folder to make sure it was what I thought it was, then closed it again quickly.

"What is it, Bill?" asked my mother.

"Nothing important."

"Discharge papers?" asked my father.

"Those won't come for years," I said. "Officially, I'm still in the reserves. They could come and get me anytime."

"They wouldn't dare," said my mother.

My father reached for the package and I would have had to struggle with him to keep it away.

"It's just the citation for a medal," I said.

"Medal?" said my mother.

"Just the Bronze Star," I said. "Everybody got them."

"With a V Device?" asked my father.

"Yes."

"The V Device is for valor, dear," he explained. "Am I right, Bill?"

"Yes."

"I didn't know about the valor," said my mother.

"It isn't anything, Mother."

"Let me see," she said.

My father handed it to her. She pulled the folder out, opened it slowly. Her voice wavered as she began to read it aloud. I didn't know how to stop her.

" 'By direction of the President,' " she said. "The President. Oh, my . . . the Bronze Star Medal with V Device (for Valor) is awarded to Sergeant William R. Morgan for heroism in connection with ground operations against a hostile force in the Republic of Vietnam. On August 3, 1970, while on a mission to secure a downed helicopter, Sergeant Morgan's unit made contact with an estimated enemy company in the village of Xuan The. . . .' "

"Nobody knows how many there were," I said.

" 'Cut off from the main body of his unit, Sergeant Morgan came under a heavy volume of sustained enemy fire. With disregard for his own safety, Sergeant Morgan held back the enemy advance with his own accurate and effective rifle fire. Wounded, he repeatedly refused to be evacuated until all the other casualties had been cleared. Sergeant Morgan's skill, bravery and leadership in extreme circumstances are in keeping with the highest traditions of the military service and reflect great credit upon himself, the First Air Cavalry Division (Airmobile) and the United States Army.' Then there are some signatures and a lot of letters and numbers that I don't understand.

"Oh, Bill," she said. "I'm so proud."

I did not want to hear that. If you stuck to fact, literal fact, then maybe it was all right. But pride was something else. Xuan The was the end of pride.

"Excuse me," I said, folding my napkin back up carefully and pushing away from the table.

"What's wrong, son?" asked my father.

"I'm not very hungry. I must have some kind of bug."

"This medal," he said. "It made you remember something."

"I'm sorry, dear," said my mother. "I didn't know."

"Look, it's probably just the flu or something. You go on and eat. I'll be OK."

I left the table and went to my room. I did not turn on the light. I sat down on the edge of the bed and tried very hard to weep. I put my head in my hands and held it there. I forced out a few little sobs, but tears would not come.

"Can I come in, son?" my father asked from the hall outside my room. I didn't answer, and he slowly pushed open the door to give me time to refuse. I turned my face away from the light, and he closed the door again and stood for a moment in silence.

"Do you want to tell me about it?" he finally said.

"I don't know."

"Mind if I sit down?"

"Go ahead."

The mattress sagged as he put his weight on it. I felt drawn to him, but it was only an illusion of the darkness.

"Something happened in that town the day when you got the medal, didn't it?" he said.

"Yes."

"Can you tell me what?"

"It was Jim Neumann."

"He's the fellow you wrote us so much about."

"He was hurt very badly."

"Did he die?" He whispered it, a terrible secret.

"He was wounded," I said.

"Is he back in the States now?"

"Yes."

"Have you talked to him?"

"He doesn't want that."

"Maybe he doesn't know what he wants," he said. "Maybe neither of you do."

He shifted his weight and I could feel him looking at me.

"Why don't you try to get in touch with him?" he said.

"I guess I'm afraid."

My father stood up from the bed and went to the window, pulled back the curtain. The moon shone through it, lighting up his face. It made him look pale and old.

"You never get closer to anyone than the men you fought a war with," he said. "But sometimes there are things that happen that can tear you apart. Maybe you think it is better to keep quiet about them. But they stay with you. You want them to go away, but they don't."

"Did that happen to you?"

"In a way, I suppose it did. But it was different for us. We all came back together on a slow troop ship. There was time to make our peace."

"I don't want to hurt him."

"I'm not going to ask you what happened, what he did or you did, because I'm not the one who can help you with that right now. If you ever want me to listen, I will. That's up to you. But I'll tell you this: The man was your friend. You can't just turn away from him. You've got to get right with this thing, whatever it is. You've got to go find him."

"Maybe I will."

"And, son, when you see him, don't just sit around telling lies. I've seen men try that, and it rips them up inside. You've got to be as honest as steel."

# 6

# Connections

The heavy weather held off that winter. The waters were still running in the creeks and rivers until well after Christmas. The light dustings of snow quickly melted, and the land was deep brown with the leavings of autumn harvest. The high, rolling clouds clarified the sky. Of course, you did not really see the land or the sky until you got out well past the housing projects and shopping malls. But at some point, not marked on any map, you reached the border of farm country. The sky was clear of grime, the clouds as bright and beautiful as any you had ever seen. And the land stretched out flat all the way to the horizon, broken only by little groves of trees and the wire.

It had not been hard to get a line on Neumann once I finally set about it. When I could not find him by phone in the city or suburbs, I hunted up the letter his girlfriend Donna Jarret had sent me and made a call to her. She was not exactly thrilled to hear from me. She said she had had it up to here with returning veterans. But I did manage to pry from her certain facts.

Neumann had not stayed in the hospital long. He had thrown himself into the physical therapy. He wanted out, but not to go to Donna Jarret. When they released him, he just up and went away.

Yes, she knew where he had finally lighted. She gave me the address, a rural route downstate. But she didn't know what he was doing there. She assumed he was all right. He always landed on his feet, didn't he?

Once I got moving, I felt for the first time since coming home that I was finally getting somewhere. It had been unnatural not to go see Neumann. We had been as close as blood. You don't just walk away from someone like that. And I was sure that when I talked to him, he would tell me exactly what had happened in the hootch in Xuan The and why. And that would be the end of it, the way it had to be.

As I drove south on the long, straight highway through the fields, I thought about the trips my parents and I had taken through the corn belt when I was a boy. What I remembered best was the tedium of it, hour after hour scrunched down in the backseat, the summer sun making mirages ahead of us on the pavement. I remembered the miles of endless cornfields, the way the tall green plants stood in ranks and files as straight as a marching band, the dull towns where we would stop for a bottle of Orange Crush and a little conversation about the crops with men in funny straw hats.

I had felt absolutely no kinship with the land back then. The smells were sour and heavy, the wide expanse of plains an ordeal to be undergone. But now, as I drove the four-lane blacktop and let my eyes drift into the calm, empty distance, I felt altogether differently about it. I remembered how Barnelli had talked on the flight back to the World about how much he missed his family farm. He had been a door gunner with the 25th Infantry Division, and I imagine he handled his side of the chopper as efficiently as once he had handled a harrow. And yet, as he described the sights he had seen in Vietnam—the peasant women leaning over the rice shoots in tight little knots of black against the green, the latticework of the dikes, the craters in the landscape too deep for anything to push up from and grow—I guess he was making a connection between there and here. And I suppose I was making it, too, as I looked out on the peaceful oblivion of the fields, the vacancy of the sky. It was hard not to feel the land was precious, once you recognized the peril.

I turned off the highway at a rusted little sign pointing east toward Martindale. The narrow road led straight as a shot for a couple miles into a stand of trees. I could see a few homes nestling there and the steeple of a church rising above the tallest limbs. Up the way, a couple of cars were pulled off the road onto the dirt shoulder. Three men in bright red jackets and hats moved through the field on line. Hunters. One of them fired, a puff of smoke appearing in front of him. The report was muffled by the open space. I barely heard it above the engine.

The village of Martindale was not imposing. The post office was just a small trailer they had set up on a cinderblock foundation near the train tracks. I probably wouldn't have found it at all if it hadn't been for the enormous flag hanging on a tall pole outside.

I pulled over and got out of the car. The air was brisk, and I jogged up to the trailer. It was locked. I looked into the window. There was a little counter with a scale on it, a bulky old swivel chair, a few gray sacks on the floor.

"Emil is out on his rounds," said a voice.

I turned. An elderly woman with a cane was standing on the road near my car, bundled up in a colorless coat, a print housedress showing beneath it.

"You might find him over to the garage," she said. "If you got something to mail, you can just leave it there inside the screen door. Emil will take care of it when he gets back."

"Maybe you can help me," I said. "Where's Rural Route Two?"

"How do you mean, sonny?"

"I'm looking for a guy who lives on Rural Route Two."

"You *got* to be from the city," she said.

"How can you tell?"

"A rural route ain't a street address. It covers a lot of territory. You better go find Emil. He'll be able to set you straight. The garage is down that way. You can just see it there around the bend. The men hang out there and play pinochle. But don't let them get you in a game. They know their cards, sonny. And they like city boys."

"Can I give you a lift somewhere?"

"Ain't noplace to lift me to," she said, a jolly look on her old face. "I'm just doing my P.M. constitutional. Eighty-two-years, three months and a day. Folks say I don't look a day over seventy-five. So long, sonny. Be careful of them boys and their cards now, you hear?"

I watched her walk down the road and across the tracks, then I got back into the car and drove the other way until I found the garage. It certainly didn't look like the center of activity. The pumps in front were out of some old Depression photograph, crank on the side, a big glass tank on top. On the crosspiece of the screen door there was an ad for some long-forgotten brand of motor oil. I went inside.

Four men sat around a table set up on the damp concrete slab where the cars would have been if there had been any business. There were crates of oil cans and boxes of spare parts stacked haphazardly along the walls, and a slick on the cracked floor showed that at least occasionally somebody must have brought some piece of machinery in to be fixed. The men looked up when I entered, but then they went on to play the end of the hand.

"You addin' them points up properly, Walter?" said one of them.

"He does the sums in his head," said another, "then he writes down how many he needs to keep ahead."

"Can I help you, mister?" said a man in overalls. He rose and glanced out the dirty front window.

"You want a fillerup, you're gonna have to turn that buggy around. That 'ere old hose don't reach too far."

"They tell me I might find the mailman here," I said. "Name is Emil, I think."

"I'm Emil Mueller," said another man, standing and presenting his hand. "I'm the postmaster, if that's who you're looking for."

"Fanciest title in Martindale," said the man they called Walter. "And he don't let anybody forget it."

"The hell you say," said Emil. "What can I do for you, mister?"

"I'm looking for a guy who lives down this way. All I know is that his mail goes to Rural Route Two."

"What's the name then?"

I hesitated to say it for fear that they would tell me he had gone away.

"Jim Neumann," I said.

"Jimmy Neumann? You're here to see Jimmy?" said the man in overalls. "Well, why didn't you say so?"

"He's an old friend," I said.

"Army buddies, I bet."

"You know where he's living now?" I asked.

"Hell yes," said the man in overalls. "He's living over to the old Shroeder place."

"You seen the new roof he put on?" said Emil. "Looks to be fixin' it up real good."

"Sure did need it."

"Pity to see one of them good old farmhouses go to seed. Built sturdy as hell. But ever since old man Shroeder died, the place just run down. Jimmy's doin' it up right, though."

"Where is it from here?" I asked.

"I ain't seen him around in a few days," said the man in overalls.

"Becky was in town yesterday," said Emil. "Didn't get a chance to talk to her none. She's lookin' real good, though."

"I wasn't so sure when he first set up with her," said the man in overalls as if it were a point they had gone over so many times before that they thought nothing of repeating it before a stranger. "I mean, these kids is different nowadays than we was about that sort of thing. But I still didn't much like it."

"You gotta say this, though," said Walter, "he's a damned sight better than that guy that give her the child then walked out."

"I'm not sayin' nothin' against her or him," said the man in overalls. "I'm just sayin' what I thought at first. Jimmy, he's a good 'un all right."

"I think he's got the right intentions," said Emil. "I don't hold nothin' against a man with the right intentions. We got enough of them around here who you'd think been brought up by gypsies."

"He's living with someone?" I said.

"You say you was in the army with Jimmy?" said Emil. "Well, bring this man a beer. What the hell we waitin' for? We let the man just stand here while we cackle like a bunch of old hens."

"Sit down here," said one of the men at the table. "What did you say your name was again?"

"Bill Morgan," I said. I lowered myself into the rickety folding chair and then dared to lean back a little on its rear legs like the others were doing. They told me not to let you guys get me into a card game."

"Hell," said Emil, "that must have been Mabel Jennings said that." He set down an icy can of Schlitz in front of me and I took a long pull. It tasted good. The stiffness of the drive was loosening up all of a sudden in my shoulders and neck.

"We wouldn't never hustle a man who's back from Vietnam," said the man in overalls, "leastwise not his first time to the table."

He pulled up another chair and began to shuffle the discolored Bicycle deck. He wet his finger before starting to deal.

"I can't stay," I said, finishing up the rest of the beer in one long, satisfying gulp. "I want to get out to Jim's place before dusk."

"Well, after you've visited with him, you come back now, you hear?" said the man in overalls. "You and Jimmy must've had some times, eh?"

"Sure," I said. There was nothing more to it than that. He did not push me or back away. He just left it there, and I could see that he knew that this was the right and proper way for the thing to be played.

"Here," said Emil, ripping a sheet from a notepad on the table. At the top of the paper there was a drawing of an ear of corn with wings and the name of a brand. "I'll just draw you the way to get out there."

When he had finished, he stood up and slapped me on the back.

"You give our best to him," he said. "Tell him not to make himself so scarce."

*    *    *

By the time I got to Jim's place it was late in the afternoon, and the sky had already started to go pink. The house was set way back from the road at the end of a dirt drive. Behind it there was a long stretch of woods, and I figured that the creek I had crossed on the way probably wound through the trees.

A ladder stood up against the side of the big old frame house. New shingles covered nearly all of the roof except for a little patch near the corner. Some of the clapboards were white with a new coat of primer, and this gave the place an odd, half-completed appearance. There were lights on inside, so I parked in the drive and mounted the rebuilt steps to the porch.

"Hi," said the young woman who answered the door. She opened it as wide as it would go and stood there smiling. Behind her a little girl was padding around in a cute pinafore. I don't know exactly what I expected to find, but the sight of them surprised me.

"Maybe I have the wrong place," I said. "I was looking for a guy named Jim Neumann. In town they gave me directions. But I must have gotten lost."

"Well, come on in out of the cold," she said. "Jim's gone out for a while. But he ought to be back soon. You look like you could use a cup of coffee."

She wore a plaid blouse and jeans. Her hair was brown, the color of the fields, and she had it braided and tied in loops on either side of her face. There was something about the face that was striking, the cheekbones and the shape of her eyes, maybe something Indian in the blood.

"I'm an old friend of Jim's," I said. She had not even thought to ask me.

"You'll have to excuse the mess in here," she said, her hand sweeping around the living room, which was littered with tools and covered here and there with dropcloths. "You know Jim. He tries to do everything at once."

The little girl looked up at me and then darted behind her mother, peeking out between the blue-jeaned legs.

"Come on now, Ginny. Don't be shy. It's only a friend."

She maneuvered the little girl away from her and I knelt down to make the introductions easier.

"Say hello to . . ."

"Bill Morgan," I said. She paused for a moment, as if she were trying to place the name.

"Say hello to Mr. Morgan," she said.

"Bill," I said.

The little girl stepped back into a corner, her eyes to the floor, and said quite formally but ever so softly, "Bye-bye."

"Pleased to meet you, Ginny."

"Why don't you come into the kitchen? I was just cleaning up from supper. Can I offer you a little roast? It's still warm."

"Sounds good."

"Ginny will grow bolder when she gets her curiosity up," she said. "They don't really know how to be afraid for very long at that age."

"She's a pretty child."

"Don't let her hear you saying that," she said. "She gets enough of that from Jim."

She made up a generous plate of meat and potatoes and a wonderful-looking casserole of vegetables and set it out in front of me. I went at it ravenously as she washed dishes in the old-fashioned sink that stood on four fancy legs.

"When did you get back from Vietnam?" she said, turning to me as she dried her hands on a cloth.

It caught me off-guard. I put down the knife and fork and pushed the plate away from me before I answered.

"It's been a couple of months now I guess," I said. "How did you know?"

"Jim wrote you a letter," she said. "He showed it to me."

Something passed over her face, but it was gone before I could be sure what it was.

"Here," she said. "Let me get you some more."

"I'm full."

"We have some apple pie. Real fresh," she said.

"Maybe just a little slice."

It was delicious, and I finished it quickly as she put away the dishes.

"Let me do these," I said, carrying mine to the sink.

"Nonsense," she said, "You just sit there and digest."

The little girl peeked around the corner and I tried to win her with a smile. For some reason this seemed to frighten her, and she disappeared.

"How old is Ginny?" I asked.

"Two and a half. She was shy around Jim, too,

at first. Now she's probably afraid you'll take him away."

"Why would she be afraid of that?"

"You know kids," she said. "They get ideas."

When she had everything finished and put away, she poured a cup of coffee for me and one for herself.

"Why did you come here?" she asked abruptly. "No, wait. Let me backtrack. I'm not sorry that you did. It's all right. Jim is very strong. Before, well, there were times. I didn't want him to mail that letter to you. I told him just to leave it alone. But he was obsessed with some crazy notion that you were judging him. Now all that seems to have passed. I'm just wondering, why did you finally decide to come after all this time?"

"I'm not sure," I said. "I guess I've been obsessed, too."

She seemed to retreat from me when I said that, so I moved quickly to reassure her.

"Just wondering how he was doing," I said. "I was worried about him. But I can see that he's doing just fine."

"I've never met anyone quite like him," she said. "I don't know whether they told you about me in town."

"Only admiring what you two were accomplishing out here."

She looked at me curiously, as if she knew that I had heard more. But then she stood up and took me by the hand.

"Let me show you what we've been up to," she said. "The living room here, it's still just in the idea stage. Let's hurry through it, if you don't

268

mind. Back here is where we're going to have our bedroom once we get to it. Be careful of these stairs. We haven't fixed the banister yet. It's a little uncertain."

I followed her up, and she led me toward the back of the house where she opened a beautifully refinished door.

"This is his pride," she said, flicking on the light. It was Ginny's room, a room for a princess. He had stripped and stained all the carved old woodwork. The walls were painted brightly, and all around there were low bookshelves he had built into the walls. The wooden toys on them looked as though they had been made by loving hands. A doll lay in a newly built cradle. And on the far wall hung an intricate baby's quilt. She said that was her contribution.

"It's all very lovely," I said.

"He really went overboard, didn't he? He wants to save up and buy her a pony in the spring. I think she's still a little young, don't you? And he has plans to turn that old wreck out back into a private playhouse." She drew aside the curtains and pointed out into the dusky backyard. There was a building that must once have been a stable and another that had probably been a tool shed. Both were terribly run down, and they leaned considerably off-center.

"He'll do it if he says he will," I said.

When I came away from the window and looked at her, she had grown very solemn all of a sudden.

"Please don't talk to him about the war," she said.

I began to say something, then stopped. There

was a force in the expression on her face that was too strong to resist, a plain honesty that made it seem wrong to argue.

"It's no use talking about it," she said. "He has never wanted to, and I've never asked."

"It must be hard not to."

"Not at all," she said. "Everybody has secrets, and if you talk about them they can turn to poison. So what you have to do is to put them away where they will be safe, where they can't do any harm."

"It looks like he's found a place where he can be safe," I said. "I haven't yet."

"Don't ask him," she said. "Keep away from it. It can only hurt him."

Just then the little girl came between us and relieved the intensity of it. She grabbed her mother's hand, cast a wary glance at me.

"Djin," she said.

"Ginny," I said. "That's your name."

"Djin," she repeated.

"She's saying his name," said her mother. "That's how she pronounces it. She learned it even before she learned her own. There he is now."

I looked out the window and saw him coming out of the shadows of the treeline, tall and only slightly bent, favoring the wounded side so little that you might not have noticed it if you didn't know to look. He was wearing his old field jacket and a bright stocking cap. In his hand he carried a shotgun. He held it down at his side as he walked toward the shack, the way we did in the bush when there wasn't any danger. When he reached the shack, he leaned the gun up against the wall, opened the rickety door and then brought the weapon inside.

Ginny leaped away from the window and ran down the stairs to meet him. I saw her bolt across the backyard as he came back out of the shack. He picked her up under the arms and swung her around twice like a ride at a carnival. Then he hugged her, accepted a little kiss and put her down.

"Please," said her mother, touching my arm before she stepped away.

Neumann was in the kitchen when we got downstairs. Becky reached him first but did not have time to warn him.

"Hello, Jim," I said.

He looked at me for an instant and then broke into a grin. "Well, can you beat that," he said, moving up and slapping me on the back. "Can you beat that. If I'd known you were here, I wouldn't have stayed out so long. Damned weasel I was hunting never did show himself. Honey, I think we're going to have to put out traps. Well, how the hell are you, Morgan? Jesus. Did you get him something to eat, honey?"

"She put out a regular feast," I said.

"I guess you've all been properly introduced," he said. "You've met my little Ginny."

"Easel," Ginny said.

"Weasel," he repeated. "That wily old critter got away again. He killed some of our chickens the other day, didn't he, Ginny? But we'll get the bad old thing one day, won't we?"

"Bad, bad easel," said the little girl, and shook her head with great seriousness.

"Did Becky show you around the house?"

I was amazed at how much he had recovered, how straight he held himself, the life that had come back into his eyes.

"You're doing a beautiful job," I said.

"Hell of a lot left to do, I'll tell you," he said. "But we've got my disability check to work with, and when I get this place going right I'm going to pay it all back with interest. Sam'll find out it was the best damned investment he ever made. Did you show him Ginny's room, honey?"

"It looks like you took a little time out to make her a few toys," I said.

"That came first, before I could do the heavy stuff. I got me a little jigsaw, rigged it up out back and whiled away the hours. Say, what have you been doing with yourself?"

"Nothing much. Not yet. It hasn't been that long."

"You're OK, aren't you?"

"Great," I said. "Never fitter. Don't even have any stiffness anymore."

"Good," he said. "Good."

But I could tell that he was not really listening to me. There was something deep behind his cheerful expression, like the troubled notes he sometimes dragged out of the chords of the blues, and it was not quite right. When I looked at Becky, I knew she saw it, too. She took him by the arm and leaned up to kiss him. It seemed to awaken him, and he turned to meet her lips.

"Say," he said. "You need a drink?"

"Sure. Why not."

"Bourbon all right?"

"Bourbon's fine," I said.

Becky left us and got two glasses and the bottle. She put them out on the kitchen table, and we joined her there.

"Still playing the flute?" It was all I could think of to ask him and still avoid the bad parts. Except maybe when he had decided to take up hunting again, which seemed too close, much too close.

"Look," he said, "why don't we go out back with this and leave the women alone. You don't want us underfoot, do you, honey?"

"It's all right," said Becky.

"Hell, I've got to show him the spread, don't I?"

"Don't stay out too long. Ginny is going to have to be going to bed pretty soon."

He picked up the bottle and the glasses. I hauled on my coat, and we banged out the back door into the dark.

"Out here," he said, "we got about eight good acres of woods, and on the other side's a pasture."

"Looked like there was a creek running through it," I said.

"There is," he said. "But even in flood time it doesn't threaten the house. Over there are the chicken coops. And all that out there is good black soil for planting."

"You going to farm this place?"

"Got a real good deal on it," he said. "Rent set off against a sale if we can make the thing pay. First couple of years might be a little tough. Got to borrow most of the implements. But folks around here are good people. They'll lend a hand. Becky's got them all charmed. She grew up here, did she tell you? Had a bad time of it for a while. But it's better now. Folks look out for her."

We walked as far as the treeline, then followed it toward where the moon shone down on the empty fields.

"That's for Ginny's pony," he said. "It's just a little piece of land, not worth planting. And back here's where we're going to put the garden."

"Looks like you've got it all figured out, Jim," I said.

"I'm getting there," he said, and without being able to see his face I wasn't sure that I did not just imagine hearing a hard edge in his voice, something as sharp as a blade.

"Everybody wanted me to let you know they were pulling for you," I said. "They all wanted to hear how you were making out."

"Now you can report," he said, stepping off ahead of me. I let him go several paces and caught up only when he let me.

"It wasn't because I wasn't interested in you," he said.

"I know."

"Is everybody still OK?"

"Last I heard."

"Tender?"

"He got his early out, I understand. He ought to be getting back home about now."

"Jones? The redneck?"

"Thompson extended. Jones is getting pretty short. But they'll be all right. They've got invisible protective shields. Nothing touches them."

"Yeah."

"Jones wanted especially to know what you've been doing on your horn."

Neumann looked at me, and in the moonlight he didn't seem so healthy anymore.

"Maybe you shouldn't have come here," he said.

"I guess maybe I wanted to know about the music, too."

He put the bottle and glass down on a stump and pulled hard at his hands, massaging the muscles, opening and closing his fists.

"That's all gone now," he said. "I lost it."

"The wounds?"

"Yeah," he said. "The wounds . . . Jesus, it's getting cold out here. Why don't we go back into the shack? I've got it rigged up with electricity, and there's a little space heater in there. It's my hideout, where I go when I need to be alone."

We walked to it slowly, not saying anything. He turned on a bare overhead bulb inside and lighted up the space heater with a match. The wall planking was gray for lack of paint. In one corner he had his tools all set out. In the center of the room there was a table, and on it lay the shotgun and a half-dozen shells. He pushed them off to one side and refilled our glasses. I noticed there were six or eight empty quarts on the windowsill.

"Becky seems to be a hell of a woman," I said.

"She's just fine."

"And the little one. She really takes to you, Jim. It's a beautiful thing to see."

"You want to talk about Xuan The," he said. "That's why you're here, isn't it?"

The truth was that I wanted to talk about it now more than ever, seeing him strong again, in love, all his plans. He was going to make it. I thought he must have found the answer. He had the key to what had happened in Xuan The, why it had to go down just the way that it did.

"I wouldn't ask if it weren't important, Jim. We've got to get it behind us."

"You saw for yourself," he said. "What more do you want?" He met my eyes and did not flinch. I do not know why, but I was the one who looked away.

"All I have left are fragments," I said.

"It didn't have anything to do with you."

"We were together. All of us. We were part of the same thing, whatever it was."

"I don't know why you want to do this," he said as he scraped the chair back from the table and moved the shotgun closer to him. "I don't know what difference you think it makes. But if you want it, I'll give it to you straight. The whole fucking thing. The way it happened. A war story. A fucking war story."

He reached over and picked up one of the shells, rolling it slowly between his fingers. He loaded a round into the gun and pumped it into the chamber. Then he put the gun back down. He paused, as if he were rehearsing the thing one last time. I thought I saw his hand shaking, but I wasn't sure.

"When I got into the ville that morning," he said, "I didn't see or hear anything at first. They were all cowering in their hootches, scared shitless by the sniper fire, by the chopper going down. I don't know why I ever thought they would be able to defend themselves. They always ran away.

"I went straight to Tuyet's hootch to make sure

everything was all right, to look after them. I suppose maybe I was careless. Yes, careless. That was it. I went in standing up. I shouldn't have."

At first his words were lifeless. He droned them like something he had been over too many times, the code of military conduct, the standing order of the guard.

"When I stepped inside, I saw him. I didn't recognize the man. He wasn't from the ville. But when I saw the rifle, I knew what he was."

"So he did have a rifle," I said. "I just knew he must have. Nobody ever found it, you know. But I was betting that he fired on you first."

"He never fired," said Neumann.

"But you thought . . ."

"The man was a VC. It was an AK-forty-seven. It lay there next to him in the dirt. I kept him covered at first and tried to pull Tuyet away from him.

"But she fought me. She wrenched her arm away and fell to the ground. She was crying and gagging, and I couldn't understand what she was trying to do. I hated the dink for making her that way. Fucking terrorist. He should have known better than to come into my ville."

His voice was rising, and I think I must have shown him something in my expression, something it would have been better to hide. I realized he did not know the worst, who the man with the rifle really had been. Or if in some dark part of his pain he had guessed it, he had pushed it down out of sight where it did its damage silently, like a tumor preying on his brain.

He looked away from me for a moment, then he hurried on.

"I motioned with my rifle for the dink to move to the door. But he didn't budge. I wanted to get him out of the hootch, to turn him over to the LT and go back and calm Tuyet down. I took a step toward him. That's when he finally moved. He went for the AK. I nailed him.

"One round to the head, Morgan. It was a reflex. Just a little tic in my finger. You know the reflex."

I nodded. I did know. It was one of the things I had learned.

But it was the other thing that tormented me. Could either of us settle up with the past unless we began with all the facts? I could have told him right then about the stranger in the hootch, but I did not. I was afraid. Maybe it was better to live with the lie. Maybe you could leave this one fact unspoken and hope that with time you could expel it like a tiny fragment that slowly works its way out of the flesh. Maybe you could never have peace any other way. Maybe. Maybe. Maybe.

"Tuyet started to wail," he said. "She was hysterical, hands out, waving them around, beating the ground. I couldn't figure it out. They were safe now. I had taken care of that.

"I caught one of her hands. I tried to talk to her. I told her that it would be all right. She broke away from me.

"Then she picked up the AK. She was trembling and weeping and shaking her head back and forth. I told her to put it down.

"But she didn't listen. She swung the muzzle

up. It was pointed straight at me. Her finger was on the trigger.

"She stared at me with eyes full of hate. She was going to kill me. I was sure she was going to kill me. Her finger moved. I fired."

Neumann was racing now. He stood and paced the wooden floor. He moved stiffly on the bad leg. He showed the pain.

"The rifle fell toward her mother. She went for it. I opened up on her. One burst. Then another. I couldn't see right anymore. I emptied my clip. And when my sight came back, they were all dead, all of them."

He stood still at the back of the shack. His eyes swept every empty corner.

"All I remember after that is taking hits and waiting to die."

Neither of us moved for a long time after he finished. Neither of us spoke. It was like being caught in separate nightmares. We were close, very close to the facts now. And we were still as far apart as men could be.

"I had always thought that I could handle anything," he said. He whispered it. The dull litany had broken, the anger had leached away. What was left was something much deeper, much worse. "I had always thought I was strong enough. You talked that shit about necessity, the green and the blue, and I thought you were just talking like a fool."

"Sometimes it's just too much for anybody," I said.

Neumann leaned across the table toward me.

"Do you want me to admit it? Is that what you

came here for? I was wrong, Morgan. You were absolutely right. When it really counted, when everything was on the line, there was nothing I could do at all."

He sat back in the chair and picked up the shotgun. He looked at it, barrel to stock, rubbing his fingers on the oily blue steel. Then he put it back down in front of him.

"Nobody would have done it any differently," I said.

"And that makes it all right?"

"You saw a strange man, a weapon. You thought he was a VC. You thought they were going to kill you. It's not wrong to survive."

"I thought I knew them, Morgan," he said. "I loved them. I had done everything I could think of to help them. How could I have been so wrong?"

"You weren't wrong."

"Don't bullshit me," he said. "It happened, Morgan. You can't change it."

"It was the war," I said. "The war was wrong. It set you up. It put you into that hootch and then it pulled the trick. And the whole thing was an ugly fucking mistake."

"There wasn't any mistake," he said. He was getting angry, and I did not know why. "I told you what happened. They turned on me and I killed them. That's what I have to live with now."

"You can," I said. "You know you can. What you thought you saw makes all the difference."

The words just came out that way, and even as I said them I hoped that he would not hear. But he heard, all right. He leaned across the table.

280

"What do you mean what I *thought* I saw?" he said. "I saw what was, Morgan. What was."

Something told me that he knew it, too. Maybe only dimly, the way you know a nightmare. But he was denying it with the kind of force you only mount against the truth.

"I didn't mean anything by it, Jim. It was dark in the hootch. You were scared. It was right to be. You saw what you saw."

But we were as close as brothers, and we could not lie to one another even when we tried.

"Goddamnit! You're fucking with me, Morgan. If you've got something to say, then you'd better say it."

"It's nothing, Jim."

"You never did like what I was doing in Xuan The. You'll never let me forget that."

"It's over."

"You just will never forgive me for wanting what I wanted."

"It isn't up to me," I said.

"Then who the fuck *is* it up to?"

"It's up to you, Jim."

And it was then that I knew I had to tell him the rest. I had to get it all out if we were ever to get past it. Otherwise it would always be sitting there between us, dividing us from each other, from ourselves. If we tried to keep it hidden, we would never be settled, never absolved.

And so I told him.

"The stranger in the hootch," I said. "He was Tuyet's older brother."

He turned away from me.

"The villagers told Apache about it after the

inquiry," I said. "Her brother had been kidnapped by the VC years before. He wanted to surrender. Tuyet had arranged with the village elders to let him stay with the family until you came and he could give himself up. The dinks who hit us were looking for him. They wanted to take him back."

"Her brother," Neumann whispered. Then his voice rose. "No. He was a VC. He had a rifle."

"His name was Anh, two years older than Tuyet," I said. "I think he was the man I saw her with that day in the jungle. They were planning his return."

Neumann stood up, his hand clenched on the shotgun.

"The man moved," he said. "He lunged for the rifle. I only wanted to protect them. . . . Goddamnit, Morgan, he went for the rifle."

Neumann brought his fist down hard on the table. The noise made me flinch. Two shells tipped over and rolled off onto the floor. When I looked up again, he had the shotgun balanced in his hand.

"If I hadn't known them," he said, "maybe I would have been more careful. I knew what I was supposed to do. Disarm them first. That's the way it should have been done. And there was plenty of time. If I hadn't been so confused, I would have held them against the wall, gotten the rifle. I wouldn't have killed anyone."

He stopped short, glared at me. He was working his way deeper and deeper into the pain now, fingers digging at the wound, opening it wider. I knew there was more.

"I loved Tuyet," he said. He was pleading with me, but there was nothing I could do. "I only wanted to protect her. . . . God, what must have gone through her mind. . . ."

He lifted the gun, held it in both hands. And suddenly I was afraid.

"I don't even know what I did," he said. "It's all falling apart. I can't remember it right. . . . Can't even *remember*."

The barrel of the shotgun swept toward me, then past. It trembled in his hands, and I did not dare to move.

"Everything was going wrong in Xuan The," he said. "I was losing them. And Tuyet, I was afraid of what would happen to us. She would have suffered if I brought her home. She would have pulled me down. I didn't want to admit it, but I wished I had never met her, never gone to Xuan The. I wished that I didn't love her so much.

"Then you told me about seeing her with a man in the jungle." It burst from him, an accusation. I could not answer it.

"I asked her about it, Morgan. Did you know that? I confronted her. And she denied everything. She was drawing back from me. But I wouldn't let go. Couldn't. It was hopeless. Absolutely hopeless.

"That morning I was all wrought up, confused. And the way we went into Xuan The made it worse. Combat assault. Sniper fire. It was so crazy. I refused to believe that it was for real. But at the same time I knew that marrying her was a dream, too, a stupid dream."

He moved around behind me, pacing near the door. I turned halfway around in my chair to try to catch his eye, to steady him. But he was not seeing me, not seeing the planking, the tools, the naked bulb. He was off somewhere else, ten thousand miles away.

"When I got near her hootch, I thought I saw somebody standing in the shadows inside the door. A man. Then he vanished. I told myself it was nothing, my imagination. I hated the things I was feeling. I fought against them, Morgan. I fought. . . .

"But then I stepped inside the hootch and saw him.

"He sat there on the ground next to her. The rifle. They looked up at me. Surprised. Afraid. I had caught them . . . him. Her brother.

"But what the fuck did I *see*? Who did I think it was? I don't even know. I don't fucking know. . . ."

Neumann's head was shaking: denying, affirming, resisting, admitting. When you want the facts to be solid, they are always slipping. When you need them to hold, they give way under your hand.

"The man moved and I killed him," he said.

The shotgun was up under his arm now. His hand was on the pump action.

"Then Tuyet. She took the rifle. Her hands trembled. She swung it up. It was pointed at me. *It's dangerous, Tuyet. Don't fool with that thing. Put it back down.* I told her to stop. *Don't, Tuyet.* I brought my rifle up, too. I didn't even think about it. It was just there in my hand, ready. *Please stop. Please let me be.* Her finger moved on the trigger. She would have killed me. I know that. I have to know that . . . because I killed her."

Sweat shone on his forehead. Every muscle was tense. This was not like the trajectory of a shell, the rule of the jungle. You could not add it up, say that what happened had to be. He was reliving it there before me, and I was with him in the hootch.

The quick movement of his finger on the trigger. The stranger. The rifle kicks with each shot, and the kick feels good and true. The smell of the blast. Its haze. The stranger in the hootch. Tormentor. Lover. Brother. He moves and he dies. The lunge toward the rifle. His finger on the trigger. The reflex is quick. The tic of his finger. The kick of the rifle. The others rustling at the edges of that death. She cries. He speaks. Maybe she hears his words. Maybe he means his words. The hootch is dim in the dawn, and living things make sounds that echo against the darkness. He speaks, but they do not respond. They move closer and closer. He loves them, but they surround him. He is trapped. He looks at her and the others, and they do not understand. The rifle in his hand. The dead man on the floor. They understand too well. His vision dims. The simple hootch is alive with complication. The rifle in the dust. The silver flute on the floor. The blood. They move and turn as he seeks the look, the words that will stop the spinning. His finger on the trigger. The grip warm from his hand. The barrel hot. She holds the rifle. The rifle lies in the dust on the floor. The blood darkens the dust. The rifle rises and sights in. He wants her, wants what is simple and true. The rifle rises. The tic of his finger. The familiar kick. The loud staccato report that is simple and true. He stands in the middle of a world gone deaf. Smoke fouls his sight. Four bodies lie around him. And nothing is simple, nothing is true.

I stood and went to him. I did not know how to

seize him back from the hootch. I could only think to touch him and tell him that he was not alone.

Then the door of the shack banged open, and Neumann spun away from me. He raised the shotgun as he whirled toward the sound.

"Djin?"

Tears came into the little girl's eyes when she saw the gun aimed at her, Neumann's crazed face. He stood there shaking, convulsed, and his eyes were shallow and blind.

"Djin," Ginny whispered. I prayed that she would not move.

Suddenly, her mother came up behind her out of the darkness. She stood in the doorway a moment, looking at the shotgun, at Neumann, at me. Then she stepped inside and placed herself in front of the little girl.

"It was bedtime, Jim," she said softly. "Ginny just wanted you to tell her a story."

Slowly, Neumann lowered the gun. He opened the chamber and carefully removed the shell. Then he turned and went to the corner, leaning the empty weapon against the wall.

The little girl came out from behind her mother and went to him. She took his hand and began pulling him toward the door. He allowed himself to be led into the night, and I could hear the little girl's excited voice telling him just which stories she wanted to hear.

"You'd better come, too," said her mother. "You're not going to stay out here in this drafty old place all night."

"I think I'll be leaving," I said. "I think maybe I ought to."

"The bed's already made up," she said. "You can go in the morning. First thing."

"I'm sorry," I said.

"I just hope you're satisfied," she said.

And though I did not even try to explain it to her, I guess I finally was. I understood Xuan The now, understood it all, the facts and everything beyond them. The war was to blame, but we were the war. Facts and forces drove us, but we gave them their mortal shape. The final necessity was choice. Green and blue were not separate. The connection was absolute. Yin and yang. They were one.

I followed her out of the shack and up to the back steps of the house. I could see the light in Ginny's window, their shadows against the blind.

"Good-bye, Becky," I said. "Take care of him. He needs you, needs you both."

She did not stop me as I got into my car. I did not look back until I reached the main road. The house glowed against the darkness of the fields and forests. And if I wept at all, it was not for the dead.